There was a bellow like an enormous bull's . . .

I looked up, aghast. A giant of a man, seven feet tall, as broad as an ox, thick-necked and powerful, swung a vast claymore two-handed, and as I gazed in thunderstruck horror, he lumbered about and charged down the corridor, eyes glazed and mouth foaming. As he bore down upon me, I deflected the weight of his claymore with a flick of my wrist, feinting at his heart and diverting his swing just enough to slip beneath it and come up with my shoulder in his midriff, allowing his own weight and speed to carry him over me into a bone-jolting fall onto his back.

I spun about and leaped past him, turning with my sword extended as I lunged at the giant's exposed throat. I didn't want this monster chasing me through the halls of this ruin. Still, I was a healer, not a killer, and I hesitated, not quite able to plunge the point of my weapon home.

The giant looked groggily up at me. His eyes, no longer glazed with battle madness, fell upon my healer's kit. He raised his hand, palm out. "Please," he gasped. "Do not—kill me, healer woman. I'll—take an oath—swear by God's secret name. I'll be your armsman—I cry mercy!"

ELDRIE THE HEALER

The BASTARD PRINCESS

VOLUME I

ELDRIE THE HEALER

CLAUDIA J. EDWARDS

PAGEANT BOOKS

*

PAGEANT BOOKS
225 Park Avenue South
New York, New York 10003

PAGEANT and colophon are trademarks of the publisher

Cover artwork by Larry Elmore

Printed in the U.S.A.

First Pageant Books printing: April, 1989

10 9 8 7 6 5 4 3 2 1

For
my husband Tex,
and the children of my fourth grade classes
each, in their separate ways,
my constant inspiration

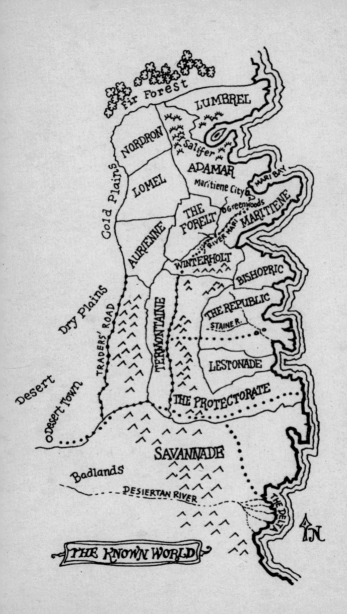

ELDRIE THE HEALER

Chapter One

✢ ✢ ✢

IN ITS LAST days, the Republic must have strangled itself to death on its paper. I dashed across rooms and crept down corridors matted with sodden pulp, the wreckage left by ten years of gaping doors, empty window frames, and broken walls. There! Another door was ahead, sullen light streaming in with the shouts and clangor of battle. I pulled my disheveled jacket about me and muttered a cloaking spell to disguise my femininity and my bloodied sword—a healer tries to avoid killing if she can—and peered cautiously through the dismal rain into what had once been a gracious square.

The fighting was heavy, too heavy. It was sure death to venture out there. The Monarchists were outnumbered by the soberly clad Theocrats, but were putting up a valiant struggle, no quarter offered or asked. I dodged back into the labyrinth of the administrative building. Pelting down one corridor, I turned into a wider cross hall with mutilated statues adorning its niches. This led into a vast, echoing chamber—echoing with the screams, shouts, death spells, and metallic clatter of battle. Here the Monarchists were winning, slaughtering their foes with the same dedication with which their comrades outside were being butchered.

Not that I cared which side won or lost. This once fair land had gone beyond the hope of triumph or even compromise. It was a giant in its death throes, tearing itself apart in a bitter, cruel civil war. It would end only as a desolation of corpses and destruction. I wanted out of this lethal trap of a building in which I had been driven to hide, and out of this nation of fanatics and fools.

There was a gallery around the huge chamber. Perhaps free citizens had once cheered the ceremonies of a self-governing state from there, or visiting dignitaries marveled at the wonder of a people who ruled themselves for the general good of all. Now it only offered a chance of slipping past the battle without attracting notice. I was no mean swordswoman; no woman who wanders the world alone goes unscathed for long without either martial skills or potent magical protection. But no woman in her right mind goes out of her way to challenge hundreds of blood-mad zealots, either. I slipped up the stairs, edged past a rotting corpse—this was not the first battle in these precincts, and no one bothered even to count the dead anymore, much less bury them—and crept about the back of the gallery, heading for the door on the far side.

I reached the opening without attracting notice, and stepped thankfully into the hallway beyond. There were no steps on this side, and I hurried down the corridor of the second floor, looking for a way down and out.

I soon found that this side of the building was heavily populated with roving bands from both sides. It made no difference whether they wore the gaudy rags of the Monarchist livery or the black-and-gray tatters of the Theocrats, they all tried to kill me as soon as they saw me. There was no sanity in them.

I fought. I ran when I could, but again and again I found myself trapped among struggling combatants or cornered by wild-eyed single soldiers. And I killed them. I had no time to be merciful. I had not the leisure to disarm them with the clever tricks my renowned and exacting fencing master had taught me, nor even to disengage and withdraw. Even worse, I cut and stabbed and slashed and never looked to see if I had killed or only drawn blood, but staggered away when my opponent no longer threatened me and ran on, desperately seeking the outside air and escape. I couldn't help the wounded. I was beginning to despair of saving myself. I was better fed, free of the diseases that afflicted this ravaged land, and sane—these advantages alone kept me alive.

I did not go unmarked, however. It was too much to hope, with all the blades and arrows flying about, even if none of them had been directed at me, that I might pass through them unscathed. None of the myriad wounds that I garnered was in itself very serious, but I was streaming with blood in a dozen places and gasping with exhaustion when at last I found a staircase that was not blocked with struggling fighters. I paused to mutter a quick spell to stop the blood.

The tramping of a considerable body of men was coming up behind me. They weren't chasing me, just running down the corridor baying after fresh blood. They drove me into action, as I had been driven for three days now, and I plunged down the stairs without pausing to consider what might await me at the bottom.

Fortune was with me. I did not find myself at once in the midst of a battle. But I could hear the clatter of boots on the stairs, and there was another body of men coming at me from the corridor at the foot of the stairs. There was danger that I would be trapped between them. I whirled and fled as fast as I could force my weakening body to move. I heard the clamor of battle behind me—no retreat would be possible in that direction. I caught at the meeting of two walls with a trembling, bloody hand and hauled myself around the corner, sagging against the wall of the new corridor.

There was a bellow like an enormous bull's, and I looked up, aghast. A giant of a man, seven feet tall, as broad as an ox, thick-necked and powerful in proportion, swung a vast claymore two-handed at a shrinking clump of Monarchists. The gory evidence of the shambles that his terrible weapon could create lay in twitching slabs and quivering hunks about him, and even as I gazed in thunderstruck horror, the Monarchist troops turned and ran, shrieking.

Without pausing in his swing, he lumbered about and charged down the corridor, eyes glazed and mouth foaming. I knew I was watching my death coming down upon me. What use would my petty little blade be against that

whistling brand? For how long could my exhausted strength stand against the sheer size
and weight of the monster bearing down upon
me?

Yet I was not one who could embrace death
willingly. I pushed away from the wall and
raised my weapon. The man was big, but there
was no reasoning mind directing that terrible
destructive energy. Sanity might again be my
salvation. As he bore down upon me, I deflected
the weight of his claymore with a flick of my
wrist, feinting at his heart and diverting his
swing just enough to slip beneath it and come
up with my shoulder in his midriff, allowing his
own weight and speed to carry him over me into
a bone-jolting fall onto his back. Clanging and
scraping on the marble floor, the claymore spun
away and clattered against the wall, out of his
reach.

I spun about and leaped past him, turning
with my sword extended as I lunged at the
giant's exposed throat. I didn't want this monster chasing me through the halls of this ruin.
A trick like that wouldn't work twice. I was
weakening, and his great weight had nearly
borne me down where I would have been easy
meat for the slaughter.

Still, I was a healer, not a killer, and I hesitated, not quite able to plunge the point of my
weapon home. The giant looked groggily up at
me past the slender blade of my weapon. His
eyes, no longer glazed with battle madness, fell
upon the healer's kit I wore slung over my
shoulder. He raised his hand, palm out.
"Please," he gasped. "Do not—kill me, healer
woman. I'll—take an oath—swear by God's secret name. I'll be your armsman—I cry mercy!"

The last thing I wanted was a sworn arms-man, nor was his oath to be trusted. But he had cried mercy. I could not for my life run the blade into his throat. His eyes were on my face, and perhaps he saw indecision there, for he spoke again. "You'll never get out of here alive without help, healer woman. Spare my life, and I'll do what I can to defend you."

I removed the point from his throat and stepped warily away from him. With a fluid movement he swept up the claymore and held its hilt up to me, kneeling before me. I reached out and touched it, accepting his oath and the responsibility for his welfare—I wanted nei-ther, yet I dared not turn my back upon him without them. "By God's secret name," he mumbled. "Come, mistress. We've got to get out of here. I'll lead the way—you guard my back."

He rose, and I found that he was not so big as I had thought—six feet three or four, I sup-posed. Still, he was big enough that I couldn't see past him. He set off down the corridor. "Stay close," he snapped over his shoulder at me. "If you feel faint, hold onto my belt."

It made a vast difference, having him to clear the way for me. I didn't find it necessary to cling to him, but I did stay close, sheltering behind him like a dinghy beneath a man-o'-war's lee. And it was not long before we burst out into the gray, weeping daylight. He swept through the fighters, claymore clearing our path as men shrank away from it. He seemed to know where he was going, for he crossed the square in which we found ourselves and dodged between two buildings. In the passage between them he turned suddenly, sheathing his vast weapon, reaching for me; I would have recoiled from his grasp had his movement not been so quick that I was taken by surprise.

Seizing me in his two hands, he flung me into the air, and I was astonished to find myself perched on the withers of a horse as enormous for his kind as my new armsman was for his. Eighteen hands at least, the great dun beast must have been, as broad as a hay wagon, and I clutched at a thick and woolly black mane as the giant swung up behind me. "Sheathe your sword, mistress," he said, grasping me around the waist with his left arm and gathering the straps that served for reins. There was nothing to do but obey. My weapon wasn't long enough to do any harm to any but the horse or the man from this dizzy height. The claymore rasped as he drew it again. The huge horse wheeled ponderously about, lumbering across the plaza and into the broad avenue beyond, where he broke into a thundering gallop. There was sporadic fighting here, too, but my armsman's mount simply plowed through the combatants and the claymore made short work of any who threatened our flight.

At such a rate, it was not long before we burst through the bitter struggle at the city's gate and into the suburbs, where furtive looters slunk about. "Stop," I ordered. "I have to get my ponies."

"Do you know where they are, mistress?" my armsman said in some surprise.

"I left them in a little wood where the smaller river flows into the Staine," I said. "There was good grass and water and they won't have strayed far. My packs are hidden there, too, with all my medicines."

"Very well. The Staine lies to the north of the

city. Perhaps we can find your ponies." He reined the huge beast about.

My two good pack ponies were waiting, as I had known they would be, and came through the trees when I called them. Graylegs and Whitenose, they were named, and they had grown old in my service. I burrowed into the log where I had hidden the packs. My armsman lifted them for me. "We've got to hurry, mistress healer. This is not a healthy land. The farther we can be from here when night falls, the better I'll like it."

"I'll free you from your oath now," I said briskly. "And thanks for your help. But I must lead the ponies and we can't keep up with your big gelding. Go home or wherever you like."

He shook his head. "An oath given and accepted isn't so lightly discarded, mistress. I'll guard you yet. The ponies can keep up." With that, he tossed me up onto the gelding's withers again and mounted behind me. The saddle, I noted, seemed designed for such usage; the pommel was low and padded, so that I could ride comfortably before him, supported by his arm.

The enormous gelding had a stride that covered more ground than three of my ponies' short steps, but he moved with a dignified deliberation that made it easy for the ponies to follow. They were used to my long-ranging strides, well rested after three days of lazing in the woods, and their packs were almost empty.

This was a matter that concerned me. Indeed, it was my current state of poverty that had led me to this war-ravaged land, along with my continual quest for knowledge; it had seemed to me that where there was war and plague there was work for a healer. I had not counted on the destruction I had found. Ten years of merciless strife had left the land almost depopulated and the few who remained had nothing with which to pay a physician, not even a stewing chicken or a pint of milk. I was considerably worse off than when I had come here; when one of the few remaining children needed help, could I refuse it just because their parents had nothing with which to pay me? Could I pass by the wounded when my medicines might save them?

I had soon discovered, though, that to treat anyone of either party, even a child, marked me as enemy to the opposing party. Since it was not my habit to inquire into the politics of the sick, I was quickly outlawed by both sides. My medicines were all but depleted, my supplies were gone, and my money pouch contained no more than a few coppers. And now I had this self-appointed guardsman and his elephantine horse to feed and care for! It was not an inconsiderable worry; they both were undoubtedly possessed of vast and healthy appetites.

The padded pommel of the saddle threw me back against the rider behind me. It would have been quite a comfortable way to ride, both legs on the left side of the horse, supported by the rider's massive arm. The horse's back was as wide as a sofa, and his enormous slow stride made him as comfortable a transport as a river barge. But I didn't like to lean against the man, and the only way I could keep from it was to lean forward and cling to the woolly mane. Furthermore, I was a lot higher off the ground than I liked to be—eighteen hands translated into six feet at the shoulder, plus the height of the padded saddle.

I usually walked, leading my ponies. The medical art is as much a matter of recognizing and compounding medicines as it is dealing with people and animals and their illnesses. I was on a constant watch for medicinal herbs and earths which I collected, and it was easier to stay on the ground and gather them as I went along than to be scrambling up and down from horseback all the time.

It was undeniable, though, that I was getting along a lot more rapidly than I could have done afoot. I was exhausted, as much in mind as body. I had been on the run for almost every minute of the three days since I had packed my shoulder bag with sutures and dressings and ventured into the capital, searching for the old healing mage I had heard was still living there.

If he had been, he could have taught me the magical healing art, to supplement my skill with botanicals and the surgeon's knife. I had heard of magical healing and its miracles, but had never met any magician who could teach it to me. So many cases I saw were not amenable to herbal medicine! I longed to acquire the skill. But the healing mage's house was a burnt-out ruin. There were plenty of skeletal remains in and about it. I had no way of knowing if any of them were his, but it was hard to avoid the conclusion that this rare and priceless magic was one more casualty of senseless war.

I awoke as the light was fading, nestled confidingly in the arms of my huge liegeman, rocked by his mount's long stride. He had wrapped his oilcloth cloak around us both; I was warm and (relatively) dry. But I certainly wouldn't have chosen to sleep where I had! I had been overtaken by my exhaustion while I mused. I wondered wryly why my throat was still uncut.

"Where are we?" I asked, struggling to sit up.

"I make it some ten or twelve miles west of the city, traveling toward the border," my armsman said. "No, mistress healer, hold still. You'll disarrange the cloak and I only just got it fixed to keep us both dry. I'm looking out for a place to spend the night, but there are few buildings standing hereabouts."

I looked about me and saw as truly dismal a scene as I had ever traveled through. Once this had been a fair and prosperous farming district, but now the fields were gone to weeds, and the farmsteads were blackened ruins slumping into the earth. There was no sign of human life. "There must have been terrible fighting here," I said.

"The civil war began here. This is the area where the Theocrats had their strongest support. The Monarchists attacked here first, and put everyone to the sword. Then the Theocrats had their turn, and on the theory that anyone who survived must have been a Monarchist supporter, they slaughtered whomever was left. Occasionally, someone tries to move in and work the land again, but one side or the other comes sweeping through and murders them. Or plagues take them. I chose this direction because I knew we wouldn't run into anyone."

It was beginning to seem to me that I was doing an awful lot of obeying for someone with her own sworn guardsman. He had yet to ask me for orders or pay any attention when I tried to give them to him. But it was true that he knew local conditions better than I did and it was very likely that I'd have ordered him to do exactly what he was doing if I'd had the information he had. "Are you a Theocrat or a Monarchist?" I asked.

"Neither. I'm a draftee. I was a hunter, come to sell furs and hides, when I was pressed into the Theocratic forces. There was nothing for it but to fight, though in truth I don't even understand the arguments of either side, and care less than I understand."

I could see how that might happen, and truly, he hadn't the look or the accent of this sorrowful land. I had never seen a man like him, nor heard his measured intonations before. "What's your name?" I asked. I couldn't go on thinking of him as "him."

"Huard."

"Huard. I've never heard that name before."

"It's a common one where I come from. May I know your name, mistress healer?"

"Oh, of course. It's Eldrie."

I thought I felt him stiffen momentarily. "Eldrie. Is that all? You've the look of the nobility about you. Are you sure that there's no territorial suffix?"

I stirred uneasily. This was a more perceptive question than I liked. Once, long ago, there had indeed been a suffix to my name, but it had carried the fitz particle that denoted illegitimacy and I had shed it with relief when I went into the world to make my own way. "Not any more," I said shortly.

"Beg pardon, Eldrie. I'd no intention of prying. There's a house yonder that's still partly roofed. Shall we spend the night there?"

"If you think it safe."

"We're not likely to find better shelter. The rain is setting in for the night."

We came up to what had once been a respectable manor house. One wing had been burned, but the central section was intact, and the wide front door stood open showing a hall spacious enough to stable the horse and ponies. A quick exploration led to a room at one side that had once been a gracious drawing room or reception room. The windows were broken, of course, and the furniture and draperies were moldering, but there was a fireplace intact. Here we would be dry.

"I haven't much to give you for supper," I worried, as much to myself as to Huard. "I could make some soup."

"If you wouldn't mind setting up camp, I'll hunt. It's been ten years since this land was inhabited, and the game is thick as flies. There's lots of farm stock run wild, too. Human misfortune is the great good luck of the wild things."

"All right," I said. "I'll clear out some of this trash and see if I can light a fire in the fireplace."

I turned the ponies out to graze, and picketed the big gelding, unsure if he was trained to stay near camp. There was a stream nearby, and I brought water in a pot from my camping gear. Then I cleared the room as best I could. My next business, while the water heated, was to examine and treat as well as I could my many small wounds. I had barely finished that when Huard returned, carrying the loin of a calf. I quickly sliced the meat and put it to broil.

"Let me have a look at your wounds," I said, bringing my medicine bag near him.

"I haven't any worth mentioning," he said. "Yours are worse than mine."

"Let me have a look, anyway," I said. "There's no reason to take a chance with infection. Besides, if you're my armsman, it's my responsibility."

He chuckled. "Very well, if you insist. There's a nick on my elbow. Can you really do anything about infection? How do you drive the evil spirits out?"

"There aren't any evil spirits. That's a superstition. Infections are caused by dirt getting into the wound and growing there. I can't always stop them, once the dirt starts to grow, but I can usually prevent them. Hmm—what's this? Take off your shirt."

"No. It wouldn't be seemly."

"Nonsense. I'm a healer. Take off your shirt!"

Reluctantly, he removed the shirt. There was a gash, starting at his left collarbone and running jaggedly across to just below his right nipple. I cleaned it carefully and rubbed it with bread-mold ointment—it wasn't deep enough to need stitching, luckily. Huard shivered when I touched him, and gooseflesh raised the hair on his arm.

"No need to be frightened of me," I said. "I won't hurt you. You don't even need stitches. You should have been frightened of the swordsman who gave you this cut—he nearly sliced your heart out."

"That was you, mistress. You're as quick with your weapon as I've ever seen."

I frowned. I didn't remember marking him, but in parrying his blade and ducking under it, it was possible. Huard was shivering in earnest now. "I won't do it again," I said gently. "It's all over now and you're well out of it. No need to let it upset you."

"I'm not upset—not by that." He caught at my hands as I bandaged the gash. "Eldrie, we are man and woman. Let us comfort one another." He pulled me suddenly into his arms, nuzzling at my face as he tried awkwardly to kiss me.

I should have been terrified. He was so much bigger than I, so much stronger, and we were alone here. My sword was with my bedroll, three steps away—as unreachable as if it had been a mile. I was in terrible danger. But the fear melted before the blast of my rage. How dared he? He had cried mercy, and I had granted it to him. He had sworn fealty. I had been trying to help him, as was my duty to a liegeman. Was I to be repaid with rape? I struck him in the face with the sides of both clenched fists and every bit of strength I could muster. "Get away from me, you filthy brute," I raged. "Is this the value of your oath? How dare you even think of offering me this indecency! Get away, damn you, you foul, oath-breaking, sneaking monster! Get away!"

Such was the force that overwhelming anger lent my blows that he reeled under them, releasing me and flinging up a sheltering arm to protect his already battered face. I leaped to my pile of belongings and grabbed up my sword, whirling to defend myself, sure that he was even now pouncing upon me.

He wasn't. He stood where I had left him, staunching a bloody nose with one of the rags I had been using to clean his wound. Over the rag, he stared at me. I waited, poised to repel his attack, ready to kill him if necessary. He dabbed at his nose, inspected the rag for fresh blood, and wiped away the stains on his upper lip.

Satisfied that the bleeding was under control, he rinsed the rag in the warm water. I watched his prosaic actions, quivering with alert tension. He spread the damp rag to dry on a window sill.

"I beg pardon," he said, and I started at the sound of his voice. "I meant no indecency or disrespect. I have been very long without the comfort of a woman's company, and the touch of your hand on my bare flesh—well, it led me to speak as I ought not to have. I thought you found me not unattractive. At least, you slept comfortably enough in my arms as we rode this afternoon. I won't do it again."

"Damn right, you won't," I said grimly.

"I have given my word," he said with some assumption of dignity. "The meat will burn if it isn't turned."

I sidled over to the fireplace and adjusted the broiling meat with my left hand. Huard sat down where he was with a sigh.

Our meal was soon ready, and I gave him the lion's share; big as he was, he undoubtedly needed it. I ate with my sword at my side, ready to snatch up. There was no conversation, and as soon as we were finished and the cleaning up done, we brought the horse and ponies in and sought our bedrolls, each whispering our own customary night spells to ward us from danger while we slept.

I lay in the ruddy semidark, listening to the beat of the rain on the walls and the steady breathing of my companion. I had laid the sword where my hand would fall naturally on the hilt, and my dagger was tucked away on the other side. I had put it there when Huard had stepped out for a moment; the sword could have been snatched away fairly easily once I was asleep, but the dagger might go unnoticed. I was determined to awaken early and slip away before Huard was aware. He was a dangerous companion.

Alas for my resolution; I spent a restless night, awakening with a start whenever he stirred, and only fell into a deep sleep in the darkness before dawn. When my eyes at last opened, the day was well begun, the animals had been turned out on the grass, and breakfast was already cooking. The rain still pattered down upon the walls; if this went on, I thought muzzily, flood would be added to the woes of the hapless populace.

"Good morning, Eldrie." Huard was sitting on his bedroll, watching steaks broil. I jumped.

"Good morning," I said warily. I was a little surprised to have survived the night, but given that I had, a deal more astonished to find him still here, after the rude rebuff he had received the night before. His nose was swollen yet. I rose and went out into the misty rain to tend to my natural needs. When I returned, I delved into my medicine bag for a bottle—my last bottle—of a soothing lotion.

"Smooth some of this onto your nose," I said, holding it out to him.

He glanced up at me. "Thank you," he said, taking it. His hair was wet, wetter than a simple venture into the drizzle could account for, and he was freshly shaved. He must have bathed in the stream. I was far from clean myself, I thought wistfully. Cold as it was, a bath would have felt heavenly. I pulled a towel out of my pack. "Go ahead," Huard said, his eyes on the meat. "You've time before breakfast is ready if you hurry."

Still, I hesitated. I would be horribly vulnerable while I bathed, separated from my clothes and my weapon. But I had survived the night—and I stank of blood and sweat and carrion and the scorched stench of burned houses.

"Go on. I won't bother you," Huard said.

I colored. "I didn't think you would," I lied, and gathered up a change of clothes, crumpled from the pack but clean, and a jar of herbal soap. And my sword.

The meat was done when I returned, shivering, from the stream, and the packs were lashed, ready to load. Even my personal belongings were packed. I hadn't intended for him to do that; I knew that an armsman was not a servant and should never be asked to do a servant's work. He was a fighter, placing his life at risk in his liege's defense and entitled to food, lodging, and clothing in exchange. I should have done the cooking and my own packing.

"Thank you for packing," I said.

"You're welcome," he answered, holding a plate out to me. I flinched at the sudden movement before I could stop myself. "You needn't fear me," he said patiently. "I've sworn the oath and I intend to keep it."

I nodded and took the plate. "This is more than I can eat," I said. "Will you take half of this steak?"

"Better eat it. It's all we have."

"I know. I'll get some flour as soon as I can, and I should be able to collect some wild greens today, though it's too early for fruits." I cut the steak in half and put the larger portion on his plate. I seldom ate meat. I was no hunter and it was too expensive to buy. I was not doing too well at providing for my armsman, I thought wryly. Huard ate both pieces without difficulty.

Saddling and packing were easily done. Setting off was not so simple. When everything was ready, Huard turned to me and made a stirrup with his linked hands, obviously intending to boost me to my former perch in front of his saddle. "No, thanks," I said, backing away. "I'll walk."

"I can't ride while you walk."

"Of course you can. You're the armsman. You can do your job better from horseback. I won't even be able to see the greens and herbs from up there, much less collect them. Besides . . ." I stopped, remembering that I had ridden before him the day before and that he had offered it as an excuse for his advances. And remembering that I had found riding so to be not only comfortable but comforting.

"You won't want to collect your herbs until late in the afternoon. And you'll be soaked to the bone unless you let me cover you with my oilcloth. Put your foot here."

I shook my head stubbornly. Before I quite realized what he intended, Huard seized me and tossed me onto the pommel. "Damn it, Eldrie, be sensible," he growled as he swung up behind me. "We can be out of this nation of death and disaster by nightfall if you ride. I'm your armsman; trust my judgment in this."

I stiffened. I was not accustomed to taking orders nor to allowing myself to be manhandled by anyone, and I disliked very much the reminder that my only protection was Huard's self-control. If his move had been aggressive, I could have been dead by now, or wishing I was. The powerful arm that slipped around my waist was an eloquent demonstration of how really helpless I would be if he chose to use force. Yet he intended no harm, I knew. The warmth of his body was welcome, and the day would surely be vastly more comfortable within the folds of the oilcloth he was arranging about us even now. I sighed and let myself be enfolded, full of misgivings about the future but unable to struggle against the present necessities.

Chapter Two
✢ ✢ ✢

"Where do you want to go, Eldrie?" Huard asked as we rode through the rain.

"Away," I replied fervently.

He chuckled. "Me too. But away to where? North, south, east, west? Once we cross the border, we must decide which direction to go."

"I want to find a home," I said, surprising myself. "I've been an itinerant herb doctor for too many years. My ponies are getting too old to wander—they're seventeen. I want a pasture for them to graze in the summer and a barn to shelter them in winter. I want a roof to keep the rain off and some shelves to put things on."

He nodded. "Any preferences as to climate?"

"Not too cold. Not too wet. Friendly people, not too inquisitive, who need a doctor and have a little money to pay one."

"South, then, once we've crossed the pass. It's
warmer there. The other things we can search
for when we've found the right climate."

I shook my head. "I'm just dreaming, Huard.
A house with pastures and a barn would cost a
lot."

"Don't you charge fees for your services?"

"Of course, but I don't always collect them.
No one wants to pay a physician much, and the
medicines usually cost me nearly as much as
the fees bring in. And there are always patients
who can't pay at all."

He was silent for a time. "Then we shall have
to work as we go, you as a healer and I as a
hunter. By the time we find the right place, we'll
have enough money."

I was touched by this offer, but extremely du-
bious. He and his mount would be more expensive to maintain than I and both my ponies
were, I had no doubt. And it would be my responsibility to provide for them, while any
money he made would by rights belong to him.

On the other hand, it was very comforting to
have my own armsman. I had never felt so safe
since I realized that my security hung on the
tenuous thread of my father's lust for my
mother. There was no knowing how long Huard
would choose to stay with me, and I was still
half afraid of him. But as long as I had him, I
was freer of worries about my safety than I had
ever been.

I was glad enough to get down and walk in
the late afternoon. There were plenty of salad
greens and potherbs, young and crisp, just at
the right stage for picking. I even found a little
bank of goldenseal, one of the rarest and most
difficult of the medicinal herbs to find, and

made Huard wait while I dug some of them up tenderly; the roots were useful as well as the leaves. In fact, I then and there bruised enough of the hairy leaves to cover the gash on Huard's chest and applied them to it, as they would inhibit the growth of the infecting dirt in the wound. He made no difficulty this time about removing his shirt, though he was breathing hard when I finished. "I don't have time for your foolish prejudices against female physicians," I told him severely. "Your wound needs to be tended, and it's my responsibility as well as my profession to do so."

"I have no prejudice against female doctors," he said, shrugging back into his shirt. "In fact, I'd rather have your gentle hands tending my hurts than some rough-and-ready sawbones."

Late that afternoon, we crossed the old border of the Republic into the foothills of the coastal range, a land inhabited by a few wandering shepherds and hardscrabble farmers. Because of the poverty of the region, it had largely been spared the proselytizing of the Theocrats or the civilizing influence of the Monarchists; people still lived here. There was even a small inn in operation in the village we reached as dark began to close in. The rain had increased in force and I was glad enough to turn in at the gates.

"Is there a doctor in your town?" I asked the landlord, once we had agreed on a price for two cubbyholes of rooms and I had turned my greens over to his cook to add into our stew and to make a crisp salad.

He shook his head, glancing at my medicine bag. "No, we've never had one here. If you're a healer, there's custom aplenty for you."

"I'm a healer," I said. "Is there somewhere I could see patients?"

"You can use the parlor," he said. "It's not likely we'll get any aristocratic travelers who'll want their meal in private. I'll send the potboy to spread the word. Er—I could have the cook put a fowl to roast . . ."

"Rheumatism?" I asked. I had seen the knotted knuckles of his hands.

"Yes. I know there's nothing to be done for it, but maybe you've something for the pain."

"Come along, then, you can be the first patient. Where's this parlor?"

"I'll sit outside the door and collect the fees," Huard said pointedly.

"Drag up that small table and a chair," the landlord said, accepting his suggestion readily.

By the time I had given the landlord an ointment of poplar and tarragon to rub into his aching joints, the patients were beginning to come in. I spent the next two hours treating the ulcers, the fevers, and the thin blood diseases that I usually saw. I did what I could, offered good advice about eating many different kinds of food and resting, and passed out sparing quantities of medicines.

I stretched wearily when the last patient went out and no one else came in. Huard put his head through the door. "There's one more patient out here," he said hesitantly.

"Send him in."

"She can't pay—it's her little boy. I remembered what you said about patients who can't pay at all . . ."

I nodded. "We've done pretty well, haven't we? We can afford one charity case. Send her in."

The girl can't have been twenty yet. She was thin to emaciation, dirty, with a wild expression on her face, and the little boy she carried was at least five years old. "I can't pay," she said, her words belligerent, the look in her eyes anxious.

I nodded. "What's wrong with the boy?"

"They won't thank you for helping me," she went on bitterly. "The boy's a bastard."

"It makes no difference to me," I said. Indeed, who was I to judge another's illegitimacy? And it was certain that the girl wasn't the town whore or she would have been a deal more prosperous than she was. Seduced and betrayed, no doubt. "Now, let me have a look at the child."

"It's this lump." She showed me a lump the size of a man's fist over the boy's ribs. I noted that the child was better fed than the mother. She had clearly been stinting herself for her son's sake.

I examined the lump carefully, my heart sinking as I did so. Either it was a terrible abscess, or it was a tumor. In the latter case, there was very little that could be done. The child was going to die. And there was no fever such as would have been present if the lump had resulted from infection. The mother watched me, eyes fixed on my face. "I'm sorry," I said quietly. "I'll open it and see, but I'm afraid that your little boy is very sick indeed."

She closed her eyes and two tears squeezed between the lids. "I've known it for a time," she said.

I gave the child a draft to dull the pain, though he was so lethargic that he had hardly seemed to feel anything when I probed the lump with necessarily ungentle fingers. Then I went to the door. "Huard," I said, "could you fetch me a can of very hot water and then come in here and help?"

Huard nodded and departed on his errand. The landlord was waiting nearby. Indeed, there were several people standing around. "Are you going to operate?" he asked, his voice unnaturally strained.

"Yes. Though I doubt it will do much good," I said tartly.

"Will you ask Cara who the boy's father is?" he said. "He ought to be told."

I looked at him in amazement. "You mean you don't know?"

He looked uneasily at the group around him. "She never would say. It has to be someone from this village. But she's protected him all these years. He must have been married, because he never had the courage to come forward and admit his fault. But if the boy—if he's going to die, the father needs to know."

"It's a little late now," I said. "The girl hasn't had enough to eat in months, maybe years. Whoever the father is, what he needs is a good thrashing, not to be tenderly informed that his son is in danger."

Huard arrived with a steaming can of hot water and I closed the door upon the village folk and their old scandal. "I've given him a dose of poppy," I said to Huard. "It will dull the pain a little, but you'll have to hold him for me. Can you do that?"

Huard nodded. "You hold his hand," I said to the mother. She must have been a mere child herself when the boy was conceived. "Talk to him and reassure him."

Huard held the child firmly, but he struggled very little, and I worked with lightning rapidity. It was as I feared. The growth was a malign tumor, involving the ribs and extending into the abdomen. I removed what I could of it, but it was hopeless. I stitched the child up.

I was just finishing the stitches and reaching for a powder to sprinkle on the wound when the door burst open. A man stood there, dressed in good woolen garments with fur trim, a handsome, well-fed man with a touch of gray at the temples. The girl turned her face away, a still frostiness upon her face.

"Cara?" he said. "Cara?"

She gestured at me. I continued with my work. The man reached out to grab my shoulder, and Huard's huge hand flashed past me to clamp upon his wrist. "The healer is busy," he said softly. "Don't bother her."

"The boy is mine," the newcomer gulped. "I have a right—"

"To nothing," the girl interrupted.

"Cara, please," the man said helplessly. "Healer, I'll pay your fees. Just help the boy."

"I'm sorry," I said. "The child is beyond my help."

There was a long silence. "Are there other doctors who could help?" the man said at last.

I'm always reluctant to destroy all hope. And we know so little. Perhaps there was a healer somewhere who knew how to halt the growth of these voracious enemies within the body. But this child had a few weeks, perhaps only a few days. "Perhaps somewhere there may be a doctor who could help your son," I said. "There are those who heal by magic. I've heard that they are able to guide and direct the body's own healing powers with their spells and by the powers of their minds. Perhaps one of those could help him."

The girl looked up at my face. "You don't believe that. You're just trying to give us hope, aren't you? You think he's going to die."

I nodded wearily. "But I'm only a wandering herb doctor," I said. "I don't know everything."

"Do you know of such a magical healer?" the man asked.

I shook my head. "I've met many who claimed the powers, but they were all charlatans. I've never met or even known anyone who had met a true spell doctor." I hesitated. "Huard, you've traveled widely, haven't you? Do you know of one?"

"No. I've heard of them, but the stories never say where they're to be found."

"What can we do?" the girl asked.

"Make him comfortable. The pain may be quite bad, toward the last. I'll give you enough poppy syrup to last—as long as he's got. I'm sorry."

"Cara," the man said, "bring him to my house. Let me take care of him. And you."

She looked at him scornfully. "And what would Aunt Ila say? She was ready enough to cast me off when I was found to be pregnant."

The man made a passionate movement. "I don't care what she says. He's my son as well as yours. Here." He yanked a purse from his belt and thrust it blindly at Huard. "Please come home with me, Cara."

She disdained to answer. He stumbled as he turned away. "You can't take care of the boy by yourself," I said quietly, motivated by I knew not what; the man surely deserved every mote of pain and rejection that came his way, yet the girl and her son—their son—needed shelter and help and good food.

She bit her lip. "Uncle Kel!" she called out. The man stopped in the door. "We'll come. Just until—until it's over." He turned, and as she bundled up the child, I gave the man a bottle of poppy syrup.

"One spoonful. When he needs it," I said.

In the main room of the inn, the whispering checked suddenly and the assembled populace of the town parted before them as they walked to the door.

Huard was packing up the medicine bag. "Your supper will be ready in half an hour," the landlord said.

"I'll go to my room and wash up," I said. I had no appetite for the promised meal, but I had to at least make an appearance of eating, and Huard could be counted upon to finish whatever I couldn't eat.

I was scrubbing and scrubbing at myself before the washstand when Huard came in with the medicine bag. "Eldrie, this purse is full of gold," he said. "Hey! Are you all right?"

It is unprofessional for a healer to let a case affect her too deeply. It interferes with her ability to help her patients, and if it happens too often it can destroy her own health and peace of mind. Yet all I could think of was the dying child. At least there had always been a place for me at my father's table. I was his bastard, but I was acknowledged and no one doubted that his protection extended to me at least as long as my mother was in his keeping. If my father's queen and my royal half brothers and sister had treated me with contempt, they had not dared be actively cruel. And none could say that my mother had gone unknowingly to his bed; she was a woman grown when she became his mistress.

That poor girl—her betrayer was her own uncle, and might have been expected to protect and care for her, not to seduce her and then permit his wife to cast her out. The child—he might have died with no one knowing his father, dead of neglect like an unwanted kitten. And even I, I who of all people could understand his circumstance, had been unable to help him. There were tears on my face, and I was shaking as if with an ague.

"Here, now," Huard remonstrated, his voice roughly gentle. "Here, now. You did the best you could. You were magnificent. I've never seen anything like it, and I've seen a lot of healers at work in my time."

"It wasn't good enough," I said bitterly.

"Sometimes nothing's good enough," he said simply. "You sit down. I'll be right back."

He hurried out of the room. I continued to scrub at my hands; when he came back, he put the bottles he had brought down, pushed a towel into my raw hands, and sat me down on the bed.

"Drink this," he said firmly, removing the towel, handing me a cup and sitting down in the room's only chair. "Go ahead, drink it."

I took an incautious swallow and nearly choked. It was distilled spirits. I seldom drank wine or even beer; they were too expensive. "Drink up," Huard encouraged. "It'll do you good." He sipped at his own cup and poured more into mine. Obediently, I drank, and he refilled the cup again. And I began to talk, a gush

of words like wine from a broken bottle. Quite
without intending to do so, and without his having asked a single question, I poured the whole
story of my birth and childhood out to him. He
listened silently, his expression neither surprised nor disbelieving, and filled my cup whenever I emptied it. I was drunk and I knew it,
but such was the force of his personality that I
drank just because he willed it. I was babbling
of things that could be of no possible interest
to him, that he probably wouldn't even believe.
I knew that too, but there seemed to be no way
to rein in my unruly tongue.

"There was nothing for me to do there," I finished. "My existence was an embarrassment to
the king. So I left. I apprenticed myself to an
itinerant physician because I liked the wayfar-
ing life and I liked to feel that someone needed
me, and I've been wandering ever since."

"I see," Huard said neutrally. I strove to focus my blurry vision on his face to see if there
was derision there, but he was only a blob to
me. "Our supper's ready. Come on, let's get
something to eat."

With his hand firmly under my elbow, I was
able to walk with dignity to the table in the
main room, where a feast of soup, roast
chicken, freshly baked bread, greens with ba-
con, and salad waited for us. With Huard's urging, I ate a little of each dish, though I
adamantly refused the wine. His appetite more
than made up for mine, I was pleased to see. By
the end of the meal, I was considerably more
sober. Or so I thought until I couldn't stand up.
Huard walked around the table, picked me up
with such casual aplomb that one would suppose he was in the habit of carrying me to bed

every night, and bore me away. I fell asleep even as he put me down on my bed and drew the blanket over me.

When I awoke the next morning, I had regained some of my carefully cultivated objectivity. I was saddened by the child's impending death, but there were always patients who died. I might save the next one as I had many others in the past. The guilt of his death was not on my account, nor yet that of his father. It wasn't anyone's fault. And if I hadn't happened along, his dying would have been a deal more painful. My maudlin fit of the evening before had done its cathartic work, and though I usually didn't go around revealing my royal parentage to strangers—for one thing, they never believed me—no harm had come of it.

There was sun streaming in the window. That alone was enough to lift my spirits, and I opened the window to breathe the clean spring air. Glancing down into the courtyard, I noticed that Huard was already up and about, chatting with a pack-train master. Even as I watched he handed the man a flat packet and turned away, glancing up at my window.

"Who were you talking to this morning?" I asked as we sat down to a good breakfast of bread and cheese and small beer.

"A merchant passing through," Huard answered. "I was inquiring about warm dry climates and friendly people."

"And?"

"There are plenty of warm dry climates. Friendly people are a bit rarer."

"What did you give him?"

"A map of my own travels. Information is a fair trade for information."

It hadn't looked like a map to me. But I
forebore to comment. It wasn't any of my business, after all.

Thanks to the gold, we were able to purchase
a few supplies, and the packs on the ponies
were a bit plumper as we set out for the winding trail that climbed over the pass in the
coastal range. I rode in front of Huard until we
reached the beginning of the ascent. For one
thing, I didn't want to argue with him about it
in front of the folk of the village. Besides, I
knew he was quite capable of throwing me up
as he had the day before. But when the trail
steepened, I insisted on getting down and leading the way with Whitenose and Graylegs,
whose surefootedness I knew and trusted. I had
a spell to keep us safe on perilous trails, of
course, but I've often noticed that the main
value of such charms is to give their user confidence; I used them but relied on common
sense and caution more. When the drop-off on
the right side of the trail got high enough to be
dangerous, and the rocks began to roll and clatter off the eroded trail into the blue-hazed ra-
vines below, Huard joined me on the ground.

There was no breath for talking. Up and up
the trail rose, and the higher we got, the farther
back we climbed through the seasons. At length
we reached the crusted snow of winter, and the
ponies breathed great plumes of steam. I wasn't
cold; the labor of climbing in the thin air kept
me sweating. My ears rang and my chest ached.
There was a metallic taste in my mouth. The
trail was almost obscured by a soft blanket of
new snow; rain in the valley had been snow
up here. I paused, wiping my sweaty forehead
and squinting up the trail. Up there, it clung to

a vertiginous mountain face, and the last I could see of it, it was still climbing, miles (it seemed) above us.

Whitenose was pricking his ears and staring up the trail. I had learned over the years to trust his keen senses; he was the more active and intelligent of the two ponies and Graylegs usually followed his lead. There was something up there that disturbed him, but he showed no reluctance to move on when I asked it of him. He would have been more nervous if he had caught the scent of a predator. Still, there was something up there.

I turned and shouted through the thin air to Huard, "Whitenose smells or hears something on the trail ahead."

He nodded, his chest heaving hugely. "I'll watch," he called back.

Up and up we climbed, every leaden step taking an effort, the ponies picking their feet up high as they waded through snow to their knees. My feet were getting cold. Whitenose was still looking up the trail, blowing nervously. The trail narrowed farther and the cliff closed in on the left. Once my numb foot slipped in the snow and went over the edge on the right; it dangled heartstoppingly over a thousand-foot drop while Whitenose sensibly halted and planted his feet against the sudden tug on his lead rope.

"Eldrie! Are you all right?" Huard called from behind me.

I climbed carefully to my feet. "I'm fine," I called back, and we went on.

Presently Huard called, "Look down! That must be what your pony smelled!"

I peered over the edge. There, far below, sprawled on the rocks at the verge of a brawling mountain stream, were the still corpses of three men. There was no question of climbing down to them, nor any reason to. They might have fallen in the storms of last autumn and been preserved through the winter by the cold. Or perhaps the corpses were fresher. In either case, we would be risking our lives for nothing to go down there. The eagles and wolves would be their undertakers.

Whitenose balked suddenly, and I was nearly jerked down by the sudden pull on the lead rope. It saved my life. A hairy, ragged man leaped out of a niche in the cliff face, jabbing with a short pike at the place I had been a second before. I heard a roar and a clang behind me, and knew that Huard too had been attacked. I dragged my sword out, dropping the lead rope. The bandit recovered clumsily from his abortive lunge, turning to come at me again, and I could see other wild shapes running down the path. I deflected the pike and swung at the man's forearm. He shrank away from the blow, but it marked him anyway, and he squealed and dropped the pike. The next man shoved him rudely aside and ran at me.

On this narrow trail, the attackers could come at me only one at a time, and my skill at weaponry was far superior to theirs. Had I been alone, I assuredly would have joined those still figures far below; with Huard at my back, I was not greatly frightened. And the bandits themselves soon realized that having lost the advantage of surprise they had little chance of harming us, for they drew off, with hooting calls from one group to the other. I kicked the pike over the edge and it bounced and clattered down the mountain to lie beside the former victims of the bandits.

Sword in hand, I gathered up the lead rope and moved on up the trail. It was imperative that we keep going. In addition to the perils of cold and altitude, now we had human foes to contend with. Night must not catch us in these heights and on these narrow trails. In the dark, we would be helpless against men who were familiar with the terrain. And there was no question of going back. The trail was too narrow for even the ponies to turn around, never mind the enormous horse.

A quick glance over my shoulder showed Huard, unhurt. He had sent the big gelding on before him—I had no idea how he had gotten past the horse—and was bringing up the rear, claymore in hand. I grimly set myself to the fastest pace I could manage. The trail had yet to crest out and there was still the descent on the far side to make.

Occasionally, I heard the hooting calls of the mountaineers, and I divided my attention between my footing on the slippery trail and a wary alertness to more possible ambushes. Whitenose flicked his ears at the calls, but showed no more unease about the trail, and I pushed on, striving to force ever more speed out of my flagging body.

Tiny red and black flecks were crawling about the edges of my vision and my breath was a burning weight in the middle of my chest when I realized that I was no longer climbing, but walking on level ground. Nor was I hemmed in by a cliff on the one hand and empty blue air on the other. I stopped and looked around. A white peak rose only a few hundred feet above me; the ground sloped up to a gentle saddle where I stood with my feet in the snow, and to the north was a trackless jumble of range upon range of mountains. I could see the eagles soaring below me among those peaks. The sun was sliding down the sky in the west, far too rapidly for my comfort. The only sounds were the heaving breaths of the ponies and the keening of the thin wind among the rocks.

Where was Huard? As far as sight or sound was concerned, I might have been alone here on the roof of the world. He had been right behind me the last time I looked. Had he been ambushed and I had walked off and never noticed? I dropped the lead rope—the ponies would be glad enough to stay where they were for a few minutes—and turned to go back down the trail. I was stopped by the distant ring of iron-shod hooves on the rocks. Presently the big gelding heaved himself into view, steaming and blowing. Huard was clinging doggedly to his tail.

Graylegs whinnied a greeting as the gelding came up to us and stopped, huge head hanging low, red-lined nostrils flaring as he panted. Huard let go of the tail, staggered a few feet forward, and fell to his knees.

Horrified, I rushed to him, opening my medicine bag. "Where are you hurt?" I demanded. "How bad is it?"

He shook his head, gulping in great ragged breaths. "This is no time to be modest," I scolded, pulling at his shirt. "Did your wound reopen or did the bandits mark you?"

He shook his head again and pushed my hands away.

I sat back on my heels and glared at him in

exasperation. "I'm just trying to help you," I said.

He nodded. "Not—hurt—" he gasped between breaths. "Just—winded."

"Oh," I said. "You shouldn't overdo at these altitudes. I feel it too."

"Had to—keep up—with you."

I shook my head in exasperation. "I'll fix some tea," I said. "We can't stay long, though. It's not more than an hour to sundown and we have to be down from here before dark. No, just sit there and catch your breath. I've got enough sticks in my pack to heat some water."

I cleared the snow away and built a little fire, setting some snow to melt. While the water heated, I gave the ponies each a double handful of the grain I had purchased in the village, and the horse twice that. The water boiled before it was really hot, though, a phenomenon I had noticed before at great altitudes. I stirred a good helping of sugar into the steaming tea and gave some to Huard. He gulped the warm liquid eagerly, as did I; we were both thirsty.

"Rested now?" I asked as I stored away the pan and the mugs.

"No, but I'm ready to go on. Have a little mercy on a flatlander, though."

Huard, I realized, had a lot more bulk to haul up the trail than I did, and he was probably less used to walking. The horse, too, weighed as much as both my ponies with a third for good measure. "It's all downhill from here," I said encouragingly.

The western slope of the mountain was wilder than the eastern. The trail was wider and less precipitous, but we dropped quickly down into a maze of gorges and canyons. The low scrub that grew a few hundred feet below the crest seemed to grow higher and darker with every step we took. Soon the spruces began to close around the trail, until in places we actually had to press between the limber, rosin-scented branches. The trail twisted and doubled back, and sometimes we found ourselves going east and north and south to get west. It took the closest attention to spy out the trail; at every turning gorges wandered off this way and that, many with dashing little whitewater streams in them. At least here the snow was melted everywhere but on the north sides and in shady spots.

As the sun went down the air began to grow colder. There would be a hard frost before morning, I thought. Perhaps that would keep the bandits huddled around their fires. I had been apprehensive since we had entered this maze. I couldn't have imagined a better spot for an ambush. But there was no sound other than the sighing of the wind in the twisted branches of the trees. We hadn't heard the hoots of the bandits since coming over the crest.

When it grew so dark that it was hard to see our footing, Huard called up to me, "Better be looking out for a place to camp! We wouldn't want to walk over a cliff in the dark!" I waved acquiescence and turned off the path, weaving my way through the spruces, here interspersed with a few lofty firs. I was careful to lead our little train between patches of snow so as to avoid leaving tracks. As I had thought, the incline rose and then dipped downward again. One of the little streams splashed noisily over the rocks at the foot of the slope; on the opposite side was a wide flat shelf with the spruces growing close about it—a perfect campsite.

We hardly spoke as Huard applied himself to caring for the stock and I prepared a simple meal from the supplies I had bought below. We ate soup, rice and raisins, and ship's bread hungrily, with great drafts of herb tea. It was dark by then, and I was allowing the fire to die down—no point lighting the way to our hiding place with a beacon. It continued to get colder, and I knew that our bedrolls would be inadequate to keep us warm. Exhausted as we were, too profound a chilling could be dangerous. There was an obvious solution, but I hesitated to suggest it, lest I be misunderstood.

I was shivering, huddling closer and closer to the dying embers of the campfire. It was necessary to speak, and if Huard assumed that I was welcoming his advances by so doing, that would have to be dealt with. "Huard," I said firmly, "I'm afraid that it will be necessary for us to share our blankets tonight. It's going to be bitterly cold and we daren't keep the fire going. That's all I'm suggesting, though. Do you understand?"

"I understand. You want to sleep with me, but you don't want me to think that you want me to make love to you." The voice emanated from a featureless black hulk, more sensed than seen in the shadow beneath the spruces. But the tone was reasonable.

"Exactly," I said, relieved at the quickness of his understanding. "Are you willing to share your blankets under those conditions?"

"I was wondering how to suggest it to you tactfully. And how to let you know that you're as safe in my bed tonight as you were in your cradle. I'm too tired and too altitude-sick to be interested in anything but sleeping warm, myself."

I chuckled. "Me, too. Very well, then, let's go to bed."

"Just a minute," he said. Taking the shovel from my pack, he spread the remnants of the fire out over an area about seven feet by four. This he covered with the dirt that had been thawed by the heat of the fire, and then with a layer of springy spruce twigs. Over this he spread both bedroll covers as a double ground cloth, and then both sets of blankets. The result, I found, when I had prepared for bed and crawled in next to him, was as soft and cozy as the finest bed in the best inn in the city. The lingering warmth of the fire radiated upward, the huge warm body next to mine provided not only physical warmth but the comfort of companionship, and I fell into a dreamless sleep before I could suggest keeping a watch.

Chapter Three

✥ ✥ ✥

I AWOKE BRIEFLY sometime in the night. The weight of an arm lay across me, there was a steady susurration of breath near my ear, and outside our snug wrapping of blankets it was so cold that the top blanket crackled with frost when I nestled lower. I sighed and sank back into a warm dark pool of sleep.

It was bone-aching cold when I awoke. Huard still slumbered peacefully beside me. I slipped out of the bed and made a fire in record time. By the time Huard woke, the stock had been fed, the fire was blazing merrily (and, as I had been careful to choose dry knots, smokelessly), and breakfast was bubbling away.

I looked up when I heard a stirring, to see Huard's head emerging from under the blankets. He yawned and looked around; a big grin spread over his face as he saw me working about the fire. He stretched contentedly and I smiled to myself as I watched the porridge simmer. Huard had done his share and more since we had taken up together; let him enjoy a few moments of luxurious laziness!

By the time the fragrant tea was brewed and the meat porridge cooked, Huard was at the fire, scratching his bristly chin. "Is it all right if I heat up some water for shaving?"

"Please do," I said, filling our mugs with tea and giving him the empty kettle.

The land had leveled out enough that we were able to ride the second part of the day. Termontaine, the country into which we were coming, was higher in elevation than the coastal lands on the far side of the mountains. A long, narrow valley between the coastal mountains on the east and the high, rugged Wilderness Range to the west, it was notorious throughout the known world as the richest agricultural land, the balmiest climate, and the most provincial folk of all the lands.

It was indeed beautiful, fuzzed with the green of newly planted crops, squared with mile upon mile of orderly farms with gleaming white-painted cottages and rambling barns.

"This looks like the place you were talking

about," Huard commented, as we rode down a lane between fenced pastures and orchards.

"I know, but it isn't," I said.

"Why not?"

"Well, it's too tame. It's—I don't know. Dull. Surely they don't need me here."

"Perhaps you're right," he conceded. "The people don't seem very friendly, either." This was true. The people we met, though they went about unarmed and seemed well-fed and well-dressed, stared at us with closed, suspicious expressions, often turning to watch us out of sight, as if to make sure we left their vicinity without stealing anything.

We came to a town at the confluence of two sparkling little rivers. The peaceful beauty of the landscape was further tamed here; all was spic-and-span clean and there was hardly any smell of horse manure. The sewer system must have run in drains beneath the ground, for the gutters were clean and dry. Tall symmetrical trees shaded the paved streets, making a pleasant fresh green tunnel to ride or walk through. The buildings were harmonious, decorated with carvings of growing plants and flowers, echoed by spring irises, crocus, and daffodils that bloomed amid beds that gave promise of a profusion of summer and fall color.

It was growing late, and it seemed a good idea to find an inn for the night. There were several along the wide boulevard that gave into the town square and more fronting on the square. These I passed by as being too elaborate and therefore no doubt expensive. The mean and shabby inns on the outskirts of town I avoided as being probably haunts of the criminal elements. I chose one that seemed respectably middle-class.

No hostlers came forward to take our horses as we rode into the stable yard, though several men dressed as such functionaries would be were working about. "You stay with the animals," I told Huard. "I'll go in and see about accommodations."

He bristled a little under the insolent stares of the workers. "All right. Watch yourself," he said.

I strolled into the inn. There was a modest lobby, leading to a public room on the left and offices and stairs on the right. The clerk at the counter ignored me until I strode forward and rapped on the desk. "Yes?" he said, looking me up and down and obviously finding my personal appearance wanting.

I had long ago learned not to take unnecessary umbrage at the rude treatment afforded travelers in some places, but my left hand clutched tightly on the hilt of my sword. "Have you rooms to rent and stabling for animals?" I asked.

"Not to foreigners," he said with a sneer. "We're a respectable house here. Our clients are either known to us or recommended by one who is known to us." He turned away.

I removed my objectionable presence from the inn and explained the situation to Huard. "It beats everything I ever heard of," I said. "An inn that won't take your money unless they know you!"

Huard shook his head. "We'll try farther along," he said.

Our reception was the same in all of the modest inns we tried. After two more experiences that mirrored the first, I sent Huard in. "You go," I said. "If I'm treated like trash one more time, I may kill someone, and there's probably a law against getting blood on the street."

From the courtyard in front of the inn, I could see the counter where Huard spoke to a clerk that must have been a brother to the other three. I wasn't surprised when he leaned across the counter, gathered up the man's shirt front, and lifted him one-handed right across the desk, scattering papers and ink jars as he did. They held further earnest converse, and some of the inn-yard workers started for the door.

"Gentlemen," I said quietly, and let them see the naked blade in my hand. "My friend is busy. Let's not bother him." I don't think they were frightened of me; they goggled, as thunderstruck as if one of the ponies had spoken. They simply didn't know what to do about me. One of them gave a nervous laugh, but choked it off uncompleted, and they shifted uncertainly from foot to foot and glanced back and forth at one another.

"Here, woman, put that sword down," the oldest one blustered.

"Why don't you come and take it away from me?" I asked silkily, almost hoping he would try it. A healer is not supposed to seek out a fight, but I was fed up. The man wisely decided not to.

Just then Huard came out and offered me a leg up, and I put my sword in its scabbard and scrambled aboard the big gelding. Huard swung up behind me. "None of these inns cater to foreigners," he told me as he reined the big horse out of the inn gate. "We'll have to go to one of the inns around the green."

"Well, if we have to we have to," I said. "We can't afford to stay long, though. What else did you find out?"

"You aren't going to like this part."

"Somehow that doesn't surprise me. Well?"

"Single women are not allowed in this land."

"What?"

"Women have no legal rights at all here. They are the property of their husbands, and unmarried women stay at home with their parents, or live with some male relative. Women may own no property, use no money, follow any trade or profession, nor even venture out on the streets alone, and when they do go out, they must stay a proper three paces behind their husbands. I'm assured that no inn in the land will admit you unless you pose as my wife. And I don't think I was being lied to, not after I shook the fellow a bit."

I was silent, digesting the implications of this. Then I laughed. "Those stablehands were astounded when I showed them bare steel. No wonder."

Huard laughed too. "No wonder indeed. From what the clerk told me, women here are meek as mice. Why they put up with it is beyond me. I can just imagine what the women of my own people would say if their men tried to keep their money and property from them. And if it were suggested that they walk three steps in the rear—it doesn't bear thinking of!"

I glanced at the sun. It nearly rested on the horizon. "There isn't time to ride out of the cultivated lands before dark. I supposed we'll have to play-act for this one night."

"I think so. Would you very much mind pretending to walk three paces in the rear?"

"Yes, but I'll do it. I hope women are allowed to eat. I'm starved."

"I'll save you a crust from my meal. And if you're very good, I'll let you use my bathwater when I'm done with it," he assured me solemnly, and chuckled when I twisted around to glare at him.

The inn in the square was tawdry and elaborate, the sort of place where they charge you double for half the service. But hostlers came forward to take the animals. I followed Huard into the lobby, my cloak wrapped about me to hide my riding clothes and the weapons I carried. The clerk was by no means polite, but consented to rent us rooms—adjoining rooms, as was proper.

"Besides," he added, with a contemptuous glance at me, "you'll want to keep her under supervision—she has a bold look about her." I'm sure my knuckles were white around my sword hilt.

Huard glanced imploringly at me. "Very well, we'll take the rooms," he said. "We'll want to arrange for two baths, too, and for a good meal."

The clerk sniffed. "All our rooms have baths. Will you eat in the rooms with your wife or should you prefer to join the masculine company downstairs?" He looked pointedly at me as he said this. I could almost hear him thinking that if he didn't pass me a hint, I would next be expecting to eat in the dining room.

"I'll eat in the room," Huard said hastily. The clerk proceeded to arrange the time for the meal, and we were led upstairs.

The rooms quite surpassed my expectations. They were almost worth the exorbitant price we paid. They were spacious and airy, large enough for a dining table and sofa and chair in each without crowding the bed. They looked out over a pleasant garden, and each one did have a bathroom. I marveled at mine. It was like something you read about in tales of the First Civilization but never expect to see. Not only was there a water closet, but there was a huge copper tub with two wooden spigots, which, when turned, yielded a gush of hot water from one and cold from the other. There was a clever drain with a wooden plug in the bottom, and when the bather was finished, he or she could just pull it up and let the water run out. The jug on the washstand could be filled from these spigots—no calling for hot water and waiting while it was heated and brought. I enjoyed my hot bath immensely.

The dinner was not to the standards of the bathroom. It was good fresh food and there was plenty of it, but it was overcooked and unseasoned. I laid down my spoon after one taste of a singularly uninspired pudding. "Huard, why don't you visit the taproom and talk to the men? I wouldn't be welcome."

"I think it might be a good idea," he said, not looking at me. "I won't stay long. Can I bring you anything?"

"No, I guess I'll just go to bed," I said. "Here's a little walking-around money."

He waved aside the coins I held out. "I've got money, thanks."

I walked around my room two or three times, sorted and reparceled my herbs, washed my other set of clothes in the tub, wished I had something to read, walked around the room two or three times, hung out the window and looked at the garden, contemplated taking another bath but decided it would be wasteful, walked around the room two or three times, and finally gave up and went to bed. I lay there in the darkness for a long time, when at last Huard's door opened. He moved about in his room for a time. Then his bed creaked and his lamp was blown out.

I lay in the dark and listened to him sighing and shifting his weight as he settled for the night, and was surprised to find that I was wishing that it was as cold as it had been last night so that I would have an excuse to share his bed again. I liked Huard, I discovered. Somewhere among the mountain peaks I had lost all fear of him. In spite of his size and the ferocity of his attack in the capitol building— only three days ago!—he was a kind and gentle man.

I fell asleep on that thought.

I was up in the earliest dawn, though I usually slept late when I had a chance to sleep under a roof. I didn't usually retire right after supper, though, and I was awake and bathed and my pack done up ready to go before any sound emanated from Huard's room, or the rest of the inn, for that matter.

"You're looking well this morning," Huard said with a smile, sticking his head through the connecting arch (there was no door in it).

"Thank you. Plenty of sleep," I explained. "How was your evening?"

He came into the room. "I had some interesting conversations," he said sheepishly. "I think there's a lot of money to be made here."

"Not by an herb doctor," I said. "Not a woman doctor, anyway."

"No, but a hunter could make his fortune," he said. "The wealthier folk—and that's almost everybody here—put a lot of store by fresh game on the table, especially when they have company. But they don't hunt. A good farmer minds his farm, and a merchant his shop, they say. So there's a tremendous unfilled market for game and the prices are sky high."

"I don't hunt," I objected. "Well, a little, for the pot, but not on a commercial scale."

"No," he said, "but I do."

"I see," I said. "Well, thank you for your escort this far. Good luck with your hunting." I turned to pick up my pack, and also so that he wouldn't see the disappointment on my face. I had always known that I wouldn't be able to keep him by me long, but I hadn't known how lost I would feel when we parted.

He laid a restraining hand on my arm. "Eldrie, I won't stay if you want to go on today. I'll go with you. But I thought we could use the money. We could hunt together. In the mountains, we'd be partners like we've always been. It's only when we're here that we'll have to observe the customs of the place."

I looked into his earnest face. He wasn't trying to get rid of me; he really wanted me to stay with him. I felt immediately better. "Well," I said uncertainly.

"It'll only be for a few days, and then we'll go looking for a warm, dry climate and friendly people," he coaxed. "And I won't leave you and go off drinking in the taproom again."

I saw a whole new Huard once we were in the woods. I had thought of myself as fairly woodswise—I could travel afoot in rough country without either crashing through the brush or losing myself, I could tell at a glance the tracks of deer from those of wild swine, and occasionally I saw game that hadn't seen me. I was a novice in the presence of a master of the art. In the forest, Huard was a shadow.

We took Graylegs with us to bring back the quarry, but we left him picketed on the good grass (he would wander in search of his friend Whitenose if left free). I followed Huard, trying to emulate his complete silence and his alertness to the messages of wind and earth.

It was venison he sought today; his hunter's divination charms indicated plenty of deer nearby. He had a little pouch with models of various game animals in it. When he shook the pouch and chanted a simple rhythmical verse, the little carven deer leaped out as if by its own accord. Huard told me that the deer were abroad even in the light of day, browsing eagerly upon the fresh green leaves of spring after the privations of winter.

I was striving to place my feet exactly as he did, for he never cracked a twig or rustled a leaf, when abruptly he froze. I followed suit, peering eagerly in the direction he was looking, but could see nothing. Glancing at his profile, I saw his nostrils quiver like a scenting hound's. Deliberately, moving with slow fluidity, he brought up his heavy hunting bow, nocked an arrow, and drew it to his ear. He remained thus poised for many minutes, and I tried to breathe as shallowly as I could. Stepping out of the brush, a yearling buck glanced unseeing at our motionless forms; the arrow sang; the little buck tumbled, pierced through the heart.

Moving with expert economy of motion, Huard bled the kill and removed the scent glands from the back legs. Then he pulled out a pack of knives and a whetstone, and, sitting down cross-legged, began to put a razor edge on his already sharp cutlery. "I've never hunted with a better partner. You know how to move in the woods. You've hunted before," he remarked admiringly.

"Not like that! How did you know that buck was there?"

"I saw his tracks down by the creek and figured he'd be in this thicket away from the flies. And I smelled him." Taking up his tools, he dressed the carcass and dismembered it. "If you'll build a little fire and whittle some twigs, I'll fix you something good." He removed the liver and sliced it, washing the blood out in the creek. Then he toasted the bits over the tiny fire I had built. We ate them still sizzling, and although in the usual way of things I disliked liver, this liver, absolutely fresh and hot, was toothsome indeed.

We buried the offal and the bloodstains. "If the deer find it, they'll know there's a predator in the forest and they'll be more wary," he explained.

"Won't they miss a member of the herd?"

"Deer can't count, and there are always too many young bucks."

The buck yielded about fifty pounds of meat, expertly dressed and packaged in the hide. Huard good-naturedly allowed me to carry ten pounds or so of it. On the way back to the clearing where we had left Graylegs, he talked to me more than he ever had, sharing with me an enormous and fascinating fund of forest lore and wild wisdom. In only one respect did I surpass him. As he pointed out the signs and traces of the wild things of the forest, I was able to tell him about the medicinal herbs, roots, and barks we passed. I even collected enough kinds I was short of that he eventually took back the package of meat I was carrying.

We were greeted at the game butcher's shop with as near to enthusiasm as I had ever seen among these dour folk. As we were unloading Graylegs at the back door, the merchant eyed the botanicals I had fastened on the packsaddle to dry. "If you'd like to sell your wife's simples, the apothecary yonder would be glad enough of them," he said as he counted out a very respectable pile of coins into Huard's hand.

"Thanks," Huard replied noncommittally, stowing the coins in his pocket. When the fellow had turned away into his shop, he glanced at me.

"Why not?" I said. "There are plenty more where those came from." Truth to tell, I was glad to make some contribution; I had just been so much excess baggage as far as the hunt was concerned. I didn't subscribe to the doctrine of simples, which holds that the herbal cure for any disease must arise in the same area and of the same cause as that disease. By this doctrine, all that is necessary to cure the disease is to discover its herbal complement and to give massive doses of that one herb for several days. Nor did I go by the doctrine of signatures, which held that the cure must resemble in shape or color the afflicted organ. But I was willing to admit that I didn't know everything, or even a small part of everything, about herbal medicine, and if the apothecary wanted to buy my herbs, I would gladly sell most of them to

him. There were a few rare ones I meant to keep
for myself, and I put these aside.

Sure enough, we got almost as good a price
for my botanicals as we had for Huard's venison. I plucked at Huard's sleeve, a gesture I had
already seen many of the downtrodden females
of this benighted land use, and which I was
picking up with lamentable speed. "Ask him if
he knows of any magical healers or spell doctors nearby," I whispered, nodding at the
apothecary.

"No," the man answered when Huard trans-
mitted the question. "I've talked to people
who've heard of one, but I've never met anyone
who had actually talked to one." He paused and
glanced at my middle. "If barrenness is your
wife's problem, I've got a formula here that's
sure to get her pregnant."

Huard choked. "Thanks, but no thanks."

The fellow leered and winked. "Prefer to tend
to that yourself, eh?" I expect I wasn't supposed to understand that. "I've got a formula
to help with that, too, in case she's a little reluctant."

"You know how it is," Huard sidestepped,
and hustled me out.

I smoldered as I walked the customary three
paces behind Huard to the inn. We were going
to have to leave this place quickly, before I
murdered someone.

In my room, Huard emptied his pocket. "You
keep this," he said. "Money never sticks to my
fingers for long."

"All right," I said, and counted out two piles,
the smaller one that we had gotten for my herbs
and the larger one that belonged to Huard. Taking a pouch out of my medicine kit, I swept this

larger pile into it. The smaller pile I put into the purse where I kept the funds for our day-to-day expenses. When I had stowed both away, I glanced up and saw Huard watching me with an anxious expression.

"Are you mad at me?" he asked.

"Of course not," I snapped. "Why should I be? And what right would I have if I did have a reason?"

"You have a stormy look about you. I'm glad it's not me you're mad at." But his tone was still a little doubtful. "I'll tell you what. Let's go shopping."

"For what?"

"Oh, for something nice. We've got a little extra money now, let's spend some of it."

"No wonder you have trouble hanging on to your money."

"Oh, come on. You'll enjoy it." He took a step toward me and for a moment I thought he was going to reach out and touch me. I shied away, startled, and he stopped. The expression on his face was so miserably hurt that I relented.

"All right, then, let's go shopping." I held the money bag out to him. He took it and stored it in a pocket. I put my cloak back on, and out we went.

The first extravagance was mine. We passed a shop that sold books, the printed kind imported from one of the semilegendary university cities. One title caught my eye immediately and I stopped. Huard came hurrying back to join me. "Would you like that book?" he asked me.

"*Encyclopaedia Medica*," I read aloud. "I certainly would. But it's too expensive. Besides, where would I put it?"

"You need something to put on those shelves you're going to have." He pushed through the door, and we thoroughly scandalized the shop-keeper when he realized that I could actually read. He wasn't too scandalized to try to short-change us, though. Huard shook the correct amount out of him and we left, me hugging my new treasure.

Our next stop was a clothier's. I had never spent much on clothing, figuring that durable was better than flashy. I discovered that Huard had a streak of vanity. As pleased as a child, he picked out a bolt of blue satin. Draping the material over one shoulder and across his chest, he turned to me. "What do you think?" he asked eagerly.

"I think you'll look magnificent in that," I said truthfully. The color matched his eyes—I hadn't noticed how intensely blue they were—and with his thick blond hair and great height he was as imposing as a godling. And the flashing smile of pleasure he gave made him as handsome as one, too. I found I was staring at him in amazement.

He didn't notice. "I'll have a shirt of this," he told the clothier. "And breeches and a vest of that darker blue linsey-woolsey, too. Now, for my wife, let's have a look at that brocade."

"Oh, I don't need any clothes," I protested, casting an appalled glance at the wine-red bro-cade he was trying to drape around my shoul-ders.

"Certainly you do. You need a nice dress. Every princess ought to have at least one dress."

"I'm not a princess."

"Your father is a king, isn't he? We don't have royalty among my folk, but all the kings' daugh-

ters I ever heard of were princesses. And anyway, you're a princess as far as I'm concerned.
What about this green silk?" He held it against
me. "Ah, yes. Perfect. Dark hair and brown eyes,
and this soft green, flowing to the floor—definitely a princess's dress. We'll take this, master
draper. Make it up simple and flowing, with a
high waist and gathered over the shoulders. And
the crimson brocade, too, more formal, cut very
low. Here." He picked up a piece of paper and
charcoal and sketched rapidly on it. "Like this.
Can you do this?"

The clothier took the drawing and looked at
it, then appraisingly at me. "I can do it. It'll
take awhile."

Huard nodded. "We aren't in a hurry. Let's
see, I ought to have something to go with it.
There, that gold velvet. A formal suit of that."
He began to count out coins, and I gulped at
the height of the stack he cheerfully handed
over.

I learned as much of the ways of the wild in
the next few days as I had in all my life before.
I learned how to set traps and snares for small
game, and the methods of waterfowling with a
reed arrow trailing twine to make it easier to
retrieve the game without getting wet. His favorite method of hunting large game was carefully to spy out the habits of the animal he
sought, and lie in wait until the quarry came
walking blithely past. This required an endur-
ance of patience that I found truly phenomenal.
Huard could stand motionless for hours, oblivious to hunger, aching joints, mosquitos, and
boredom, then flash into instant action when his
game finally appeared. Or he could give up
without chagrin when night fell or it began to

rain and it became clear that his luck was out for the day. "It happens," he'd say with a shrug and a grin. "The wild things have their own reasons."

He could carry without apparent effort burdens that I would have hesitated to load onto one of my ponies. But he generally could not walk so far or so fast as I could in a day. He tired easily when pressed to great speeds, and I realized that the huge horse that he rode was a necessity and not a luxury for him.

I eagerly absorbed the lessons he had to teach. Once we went our separate ways, I could foresee many a toothsome meal obtained by the skills he imparted. But he was not a teacher who stood upon his dignity; he was as eager to learn what I had to tell of the plants of the forest and plain, the medicinal herbs, and the many edible greens and roots. Our days, when not actively engaged in the hunt, were a pleasurable round of sharing information and congenial conversation.

We philosophized a good deal. Huard explained to me his people's concept of the harmony of nature. "There is a place for every kind of creature and plant," he told me. "Each sort is provided with its proper food and with its proper enemies, too, so that it doesn't outbreed and destroy its food supply, or become so thick that plagues strike it. Only mankind is outside this system. The wolves take the weak and sickly among the deer. That way, the herd is improved in the next generation. But human hunters take the best and strongest, and the herd dwindles and dies. People have no sense of their proper place in the order nor have they enemies that keep their numbers thinned."

"I'm not so sure of that," I retorted. "Wasn't there a drastic thinning going on in the Republic when we escaped? It's true that the brave and warlike are most often killed in war, but who's to say the human herd isn't better off without them? We're as much a part of nature as any wolf pack."

"Animals rely on instinct rather than reason to guide their actions," he said. We were dressing a large kill of northern-bound ducks, and arguing amiably while up to our elbows in feathers.

"I've never noticed that people reason much either," I said. "It seems to me that most people react on a basis of feeling. Why else would the people of this place, which surely must be one of the fairest in the known world, treat each other with such humorless coldness? The women tolerate treatment I wouldn't inflict upon one of my ponies, and the men deny themselves the intelligent companionship of their women because they're afraid they'll lose control of them if they're competent to take care of themselves."

"And they're right, too. So who's to say that for them their way is wrong? I wouldn't like it—I feel like a complete jackass swaggering down the street in front of you—but they seem happy in their customs." Huard was a man of large tolerance.

"Maybe," I said doubtfully. "I am loathe having to walk behind you. I'd rather walk alone."

"It's only for a few more days," he reassured me. "As soon as our new clothes are finished and we have a little extra money saved up, we'll be moving on and I'll be taking your orders meekly again."

I snorted. "Again? When was the first time?"

He grinned amiably at me. "Well, in an emergency situation, doesn't your father follow the advice of his bodyguards?"

"He doesn't have bodyguards. He says that a king who can't walk among his people without fear of assassination probably deserves to be assassinated—and he's a formidable armsman himself. But I suppose when he does have them, when visiting another country or something, he listens to them if the need arises."

"How did he feel about you leaving?"

"I'm not sure he noticed. My mother had fallen from favor years before and married a wealthy merchant. I remained in the palace when my mother left, but my father seldom even spoke to me after that, and I wasn't sure whether my mother left me there because the king wanted her to or because her new husband wouldn't have me. If I had been given something to do, something useful, I'd have thought that perhaps I was needed, but there wasn't any work for me." I glanced over at my companion. He was cleaning the ducks with expert strokes, listening to me attentively. "Do you know, you're the first person I ever told this to that believed me?"

"Why shouldn't I? You've never lied to me. Perhaps you weren't given any work because you were a princess."

"I wasn't a princess. Only a queen's daughter is a princess. I was an acknowledged bastard, that's all. My father could have given me a title; he chose not to."

"Then maybe you were too young to be given a job."

"I was sixteen. That's old enough to be useful. I even asked if I might help in the stables— I was mad for horses as young girls are—but they didn't need another pair of hands, they said."

"When we leave here, let's go back to your father's kingdom."

"What for?" I had twisted and turned in my wanderings for all these years, but never had my steps taken me back to my birthplace. I never intended to return.

"To see your father. To find out if you're needed there. You've got royal blood. Certain responsibilities go with that."

I flushed. "I don't need you to point out my responsibilities. My royal blood has never done anything for me. And how would I get in to visit my father? He probably wouldn't recognize me."

"He has four children. Could a man forget his own child? He certainly isn't so old he's senile. He can't have been much over thirty-five when you ran away."

"Not as much, I think. How did you know that?"

"Oh," he said casually, "you told me, back in the village on the other side of the pass."

I eyed him doubtfully, but his face was innocent of guile. I didn't remember telling him, but I had been very upset. Who knew what I'd babbled? And how else would he have known? My father had been married very young to a girl he had never met until his wedding day—he had been seventeen and she fourteen—and she had borne him three children in quick and grudging succession. When she found herself pregnant for the third time, she had turned her young and ardent husband out of her bed, in favor (it was said) of her true sweetheart. Several sentimental ballads had been written about the touching devotion of this adulterous couple, and I had never noticed that my father minded much. I had been born less than three months after my younger half-brother. Let's see, the king must be about fifty-one now. Why, that wasn't old at all!

Huard was packing up the ducks now, wrapping them in cool damp leaves and placing them in the packs. We had Whitenose with us today, and he was sidling around making a nuisance of himself. I went to his head to steady him. "No," I said decidedly.

"Eh?"

"No, we aren't going to my father's kingdom. I've made my way in the world outside it. I'm happy and useful and they've been getting along without me this long; they can just continue to do so."

"Very well," he said good-naturedly. "It was just a thought."

Chapter Four

✤ ✤ ✤

THERE WAS A delegation waiting for us—rather, for Huard—when we got to the game butcher's shop.

"We hear that you're a hunter," said the spokesman, a small nervous man with the dour expression common to the folk of this fair and smiling land.

Huard handed the butcher the last of the ducks and tucked away the money before answering. "As you see," he said. The friendly openness I saw in him was gone; he was as grim and laconic as the men who accosted him.

"We have work for a hunter, if you care for the job," the man said.

Huard waited. At last the man said, "We have a rogue wild boar that's doing a deal of damage to our crops. We'd pay a good sum to the hunter who brought the beast down."

"How good a sum?"

The man named an amount of money that Huard and I working together would have had trouble earning in a week, selling game and botanicals. Huard only shrugged. "I can do as well here," he said. "Boars are dangerous."

"Afraid, are you?"

Huard glanced contemptuously at him. The man shifted nervously, then named a higher price. "Whereabouts is this boar?" Huard asked.

We had been hunting and gathering in the mountains out of which we had ridden. The town we were staying in was only about six miles away from them, but the Wilderness

Range, far more wild and rugged, was over twenty miles away. These men came from Granton, a town under the very eaves of the primeval forest that spilled down out of the Wilderness Range, and quite a bit farther to the south.

"That's two days' journey just to get there," Huard said, "and lodging while I get to know the country—a week at least. And two days' journey back."

The spokesman looked even more sour. He canvassed his party by eye, then turned back to Huard. "Very well. Expenses for four days' travel and lodging for a week in Granton."

"For myself and my wife."

The man looked shocked. "We certainly wouldn't expect you to leave your wife behind, to fall prey to any passing male. Of course you and your wife."

Huard glanced at me and I shrugged imperceptibly. "Very well," he said. "We'll set out in the morning."

"We needn't come back here," I said to Huard when we reached the privacy of our rooms. "We could just go on south from Granton when we get the boar."

"They don't need to know that," he pointed out gently. "These folk don't respect you unless you cheat them roundly. I'll go to the clothier's and see about our new clothes. They should be ready by now. Do you want to come?"

"No, I've had enough of meek subservience for one day. I'll stay and read." My *Encyclopaedia Medica* was a weighty tome indeed, in more than poundage, but I was plowing through it determinedly. I disagreed with some of what I read, but also learned much that would make me a better healer.

Huard grinned. "All right, but I've got to tell you that I don't like the way you look at me sometimes when you've been reading that book. I warn you fairly: no curing me of diseases I haven't got!"

I laughed. I *had* once or twice speculated upon dosing him for some ailment I hadn't even suspected he had until I read of it. For example, it had come as a revelation to me that men of ruddy coloration were more prone to strokes than paler ones, and Huard was possessed of what, until I read that, I had considered a healthy color under his tan. I had contemplated briefly treating him with a preventive dose of bugwort, but I had never been very convinced of the plant's efficacy in the first place, and in the second place, I knew of my own experience that it was men of irascible and impatient temperament who were at risk of apoplexies. You couldn't have found a more easygoing and less impatient man than Huard if you'd searched for a year. "I promise," I said. "You're safe from my experiments."

I was laboring through a treatise on how to identify born criminals by the shape of their skulls (nonsense, and pernicious nonsense at that) when Huard returned carrying parcels. I laid my book aside. "How many pieces do those clothes come in?" I asked, eyeing the mound of packages he deposited on the table. And here came a delivery boy, following him with even more boxes and string-wrapped parcels. And another!

"There were a few little things we needed that

I thought I might as well pick up while I was out," he said airily. "Come and look."

He hadn't given me the money that the game butcher had given him for the ducks, I realized. But I couldn't find it in my heart to mention it. He had obviously had a marvelous time spending it, from the sparkle in his eye and the flush in his cheeks, and was looking forward eagerly to the excitement of showing me his acquisitions. Besides, it was his money to do as he liked with. I couldn't help but wonder what was going to become of him in his old age, with no one to look after him and no money saved.

I came to the table and sat down. Huard began picking up one parcel after another, feeling them, and sorting them into piles. "Here," he said, handing me a small flat one. "Open this."

I did so. It was a lovely soft scarf, the filmy kind that can be worn on the head, or around the neck to embellish a plain dress, or around the waist as a belt. It was rose-pink with golden fringes. "It's beautiful," I said, examining it. It was also absolutely useless for any practical purpose whatsoever.

"Try it on," Huard prompted. I put it around my neck and tied it loosely. "There," he crowed. "I knew it would look beautiful on you."

There was nothing to do but to thank him graciously. He opened a package, revealing a tooled leather belt with a silver buckle for himself, and handed me another package. It was a fur muff. "Huard . . ." I said, looking at this dubiously. A fur muff! For an itinerant herbalist!

"It'll come in handy this winter," he said. "Here." He handed me another package, which proved to contain three silk blouses, blue, green, and primrose, delicately embroidered with botanical designs. "I thought you might like these, as fond of herbs as you are," he explained.

I held up the blue one. "They're beautiful," I said. "You certainly do have exquisite taste. But, Huard, how am I to get them on?" They buttoned up the back, each with about forty tiny little buttons.

He coughed, cleared his throat. "I could fasten them for you," he offered, blushing. "Now don't take me wrong, I don't mean anything indecent."

"Even I," I reassured him, "don't consider buttons indecent. But you won't be there to fasten them forever, you know."

He was opening another package—crisp white linen shirts for himself, each decorated with a bit of lace at the throat and cuff. "What do you think?" he asked, holding one up to his chest.

"You'll look very handsome," I said.

"You need something to wear with your new blouses," he said, handing me a bulky parcel. In it were skirts, full and flowing, chosen to match the blouses. They were long enough to touch the floor, midnight blue, sage green, and old gold. Plain and simple, but of the very finest cloth, they would complement the silk blouses to perfection.

"I—thank you, Huard, but—"

He put another package into my hands. Matching kidskin belt and heeled slippers, of course.

"Huard!" I said.

"Don't you like them?" he said, putting on a hurt expression.

"Of course I like them. And I think it was incredibly kind of you to buy them for me. But I don't need them!"

"It's all right to own some things you don't need."

"Not when you live as I do. Where do you think I'm going to wear all these beautiful things? Gathering mushrooms?"

He was holding a last box, the smallest one. He looked down at it uncertainly. "I hoped you'd be pleased," he said wistfully. "You have so few pretty things, and you deserve them. I don't mean to be presumptuous, but I'd enjoy very much seeing you dressed in these things, and I hoped that you'd enjoy pleasing me by dressing in them."

I felt like the smallest and meanest worm on earth. "Oh, Huard, I would love to wear them," I cried impulsively. "Forgive me. I've never owned such nice things, and I'm used to thinking only of serviceability in my clothes. If it would please you, I'll wear them here in the room."

He looked up at me, smiling in delight. "Would you really wear them for me?" he said. "There's one more thing you haven't seen—the rest are the clothes we ordered. Here." He handed me the box he held.

It was about the size of a glove box, and I assumed that that was what it was. I opened it, prepared to compliment him on choosing one practical item. Instead, my jaw dropped as I found myself looking at a set of gold filigree jewelry. There was a pectoral, earrings, bracelet, hair clip, and a ring, all cunningly wrought of fine gold wire to incorporate a design of fantastic plants and animals, twining and twisting about one another in an exuberant dance of joyous life and procreation. It was a princely gift. I couldn't possibly accept such a thing. As I stared at it in awe, I began to realize how cleverly I had been manipulated. For I couldn't refuse it, either, not after having made my protest and backed down with apologies.

I looked up at him, groping for the right words to say. He was watching me with a faint anxiety in his eyes. He knew as well as I did that the jewelry was an unacceptably splendid gift. He also knew what a difficult position he had put me in. "Where in this benighted land of withered souls did you find this?" I asked.

He smiled. "I stopped in the jeweler's—there was a stickpin in the window I liked—and he showed me this. He couldn't sell it here, he said; the folk of Termontaine would consider it obscene. And he couldn't bear to melt it down for the gold, since it was so beautiful. He thought that since I was a barbarian from over the mountains, I might buy it. He asked a low price, almost nothing. And I knew when I saw it that it was meant to belong to you."

I looked back down at it. "Huard," I said, "you know I can't accept it. It's too magnificent. It's too beautiful. It's too—well, it's the sort of thing a man gives his—well, his—"

"His wife?"

"Yes, but only if his wife is also his mistress and his best friend," I said, touching the incredible delicacy of the work. "Not a wife that has been forced on him. I'll wear it, if you like, as long as we're together. But when we part, you must take it. I hope that someday you'll find the woman to whom this really does belong."

"And I hope that someday you find the man from whom you would have accepted it," he

said gravely. "Very well, Eldrie. If you won't
have it as a gift, then take it as a loan."

"I will. Thank you for understanding why I
couldn't accept it."

"Here's the green silk gown," he said. "Will
you wear the set with it tonight for dinner?"

I took the package. "Yes. And thank you for
all the beautiful things."

He nodded gravely. "You're welcome. It was
my pleasure to buy them for you. And if you
feel misgivings about accepting gifts from your
sworn armsman, remember that I bought them
with our money."

Huard had bought a deck of cards and taught
me a complex gambling game from his own
land. We played most evenings, and all our
combined funds had moved back and forth between us so often that we just split whatever
amount we had at the beginning of each evening's play and referred to all the money as
"ours." I was keeping close track of the amount
Huard earned with his hunting, though, so that
I could return it to him when we parted. Living
expenses were so high here that it would leave
me more or less destitute, but that was one of
the responsibilities I had accepted when I
reached out and touched his sword hilt. Anyway, I was no stranger to poverty.

When I bathed, I washed my hair and rinsed
it with a lukewarm tea of lemon grass, laven-
der, and rosemary. This darkened the color a
little and made it fuller and shinier. I fluffed it
with my fingers as it dried—not a long time,
since I kept it short for comfort and convenience. Then I put on the dress, dabbed a little
rouge cream (I kept it to sell) on lip and cheek,

darkened my lashes and brows, and went into the bedroom to get the jewelry.

The bracelet slipped easily onto my wrist and the ring was made as if to fit the forefinger of my right hand. The holes in my earlobes were still open, though I hadn't worn earrings for many years, and the earrings dangled richly against the angle of my jaw. The hair clip I put in my newly fluffy hair over my ear and let it peep through the curls. I was examining the clasp on the pectoral when I heard a soft step behind me and turned to see Huard, dressed in his gold velvet suit, freshly shaven and magnificent. He looked far more princely than my half-brothers, both of whom took after the queen and were indifferent in stature, with sharp features.

"The jeweler showed me how to work the clasp. Shall I help you?" he said.

"Please," I said, handing it to him and turning my back. I heard him take an indrawn breath, and then the cool gold was laid against my skin and I could feel his fingers at the nape of my neck. They trembled a little as he fastened the clasp. His hands dropped when the task was done, but he didn't step away from me, and in my turn I trembled, my skin prickling all over. I was exquisitely sensitive to his invisible closeness; he radiated presence as a great fire radiates heat. It was too much, too strong; I stepped forward quickly, and turned to face him from a safe distance.

There was an expression on his face I hadn't seen before, a kind of fine-drawn intensity. "Eldrie, you are beautiful," he said, a husky rasp in his voice.

"Not so beautiful as you are!" I exclaimed,

with more truth than elegance. And it was true. Golden hair, deeply blue eyes, a powerful, symmetrical figure, he was at that moment the most beautiful human being I had ever seen. In his everyday hunting clothes, he was distinguished more for his kindly, good-natured countenance then for any regularity of feature; dressed in his splendid new costume and with that keen intensity of expression, he was magnificent.

He laughed, and the good humor returned to his face. "Yes, indeed, quite a pair, we are," he said. "These poor pinched folk will never know what a splendid treat they're missing by not allowing themselves a chance to look at us."

The waiter who came to deliver our dinner entered at that moment and reacted most gratifyingly. He sidled through the door with his tray. Turning, he saw us, standing by the table in our finery, laughing. His mouth fell open and he nearly dropped our dinner. Glancing from one to the other of us, he made haste to set the table and put our food upon it. Then he scurried out.

Neither of us made a very good meal. I was thoroughly tired of the bland food offered here, and I felt very strange, as if I hardly knew myself. We spoke of the ordinary things of our lives, but as if we were strangers repeating set lines. The air was full of tension, though I couldn't identify its source. We played cards afterward with a kind of distracted absentmindedness, and at last I laid down my cards.

"I'll be glad to get back to being my plain old self," I said with a sigh. "I like us better when we aren't so magnificent that we can hardly stand ourselves."

"Do you think that's it?" Huard inquired. He

was watching me with that strange intentness again.

"What else can it be? We aren't sickening for something, are we?"

"No," he said, the expression disappearing. "I believe I'll go to bed. We'll want to be on the road early in the morning. Shall I unfasten the pectoral before I go?"

Somehow, I was reluctant to let him. All this awkwardness had started when I had let him fasten it. But he was already coming around the table. Anyway, I didn't know how to unfasten it, and I certainly didn't want to take a chance of damaging it.

When his hand brushed my shoulder, I shuddered. He had some difficulty finding the clasp, for his fingers moved over my bare neck for what seemed a very long time before they busied themselves with their work. I discovered that I wasn't breathing, and gasped in a lungful of air. Then the clasp opened, and he was handing me the pectoral and bidding me good-night. I sat at the table for a time after he was gone.

It was quite a lengthy chore to pack. All our new possessions had to be put away with due consideration for wrinkles and stains, and we wrangled amiably as we put this here and that there. The flat box with the jewelry in it I insisted on carrying in my medicine bag, which never left my person while I was traveling. The ponies knew we were moving on, and were glad of it; Whitenose, disregarding his venerable years, pranced a little as we loaded him and threw the hitch over his pack.

Huard offered his cupped hands, and I was boosted to my place on the pommel of his saddle. The folk of the inn actually came out to bid us farewell, and I saw the waiter, peering suspiciously at us. But we had returned to our mundane comfortable selves, travel-worn and a little ragged, with no hint of the magnificence of the evening before, and he turned away, disappointed.

"Let me down, I want to walk," I said, once we were out of the town and traveling down one of the tree-shaded highways. I was conscious of a lifting of spirits to be on the road again, even though I knew we weren't leaving Termontaine, and I wanted to feel the road under my feet and the pleasurable flexing of muscles too long constrained from free action.

"Ride with me a little farther," Huard said.

"Why?"

"If you won't ride, I'll have to walk too. I didn't like it when you walked three paces behind me; how do you think I'd feel riding down the road in lordly state while you trudged along behind?"

I hadn't considered the matter in that light. I could see that he might feel that way. Walking was more of a labor for him than for me. And if he walked too, we'd have to stop more frequently and for longer rests. "Very well," I said reluctantly, "but I don't like that saddle. It throws me back against you. Why is it built like that?"

"Well, we don't keep many horses in my homeland and they often have to provide transportation for more than one rider."

"But wouldn't it be more practical to have a pillion behind the saddle?"

"Some of them are arranged like that, but this is a courting saddle. They say that if a man and woman ride a mile together on a saddle like this, they might as well get married."

I struggled between amusement and embarrassment. "Knowing that, it would be inexcusable of me to tease you by riding with you."

"I promise not to take your closeness as teasing," he said with a smile. "Or maybe you could learn to like riding with me."

It was a very uncomfortable ride. I kept leaning forward, which threw me out of the horse's rhythm.

At last Huard sighed. "Eldrie, for heaven's sake lean back. I'm not going to do anything to you. Damn it, I gave you my promise."

"I know," I said. "It isn't you, it's me. It seems wanton to lean against you."

"I know—none better!—that you aren't a wanton. Lean back. Rest your head on my shoulder. It won't hurt you to relax a little."

I let myself slide back in the saddle, although I did not put my head on his shoulder. I was so fatigued with struggling to keep forward that I was going to have to lean back soon anyway— this was a lot more effort than walking. I rested against his chest, alert for any indication that my action might be misunderstood. After a time, the tension faded from my muscles. His arm closed a little more snugly about my middle; he was relaxing too. It was going to be all right.

Exhausted more with the emotional strains of the day than the physical effort, we spent the night in a small inn in a little village along the way. Away from the larger towns, the people were a little friendlier. I even had a patient. After supper, there came a shy tapping on the door. When Huard opened it, a blushing girl stood there, her male escort hovering uncomfortably in the background.

"Are you the woman healer?" she whispered, in an agony of embarrassment.

"Yes," I said, glancing at Huard. He turned to the man, who was nearly as red as the girl.

"Come out to the taproom and have a drink," he invited genially. "I can see we aren't wanted here."

It wasn't much, a minor infection of the genitalia. I gave her a cream to rub in and some advice about cleanliness. "Newly married?" I asked.

"A month ago," she whispered, blushing yet again.

"And your husband was a virgin too, I'll bet." This reduced her to complete confusion. "Was that him with you?" She nodded. "Wait here."

I put my head in the taproom and caught Huard's eye. "Er, Huard," I said, blushing a little myself, "would you have a word with that young man? They're newly married, and he's being too rough with her. I don't think either one of them has the foggiest idea what they're doing."

"You want *me* to tell him the facts of life?"

"Yes, please. Tell him that he needs to be gentle and affectionate and not hurry her. He needs to be sure she's ready for him." I gave him a close look. "You do know what I'm talking about, don't you?"

"I certainly do appreciate your faith in my expertise," he said dryly. "Considering the way you feel about me yourself."

"I don't have any qualms about your skills," I said with dignity. "Will you talk to him?"

"Fortified by that testimonial, could I do anything else?" He retreated across the taproom, and I saw him lay his hand upon the man's shoulder and lead him out of the room, presumably in search of privacy.

They were gone for quite a long time, and I used the opportunity to give the girl a lecture on pleasing a man and how to get him to please her. She was incredulous at first—it had apparently never occurred to her that married love was supposed to be pleasurable—but she was soon absorbing information avidly.

There was a tapping on the door. "But not," I finished hastily, "for a week or two—until the pain is gone." I let her out to join her husband, noting that they both blushed when they saw one another.

"Whew," Huard whistled, wiping his forehead theatrically when the door closed behind him. "It was touch and go there for a while. I didn't know if the lad was going to throw a punch at me or faint."

I grinned. "Which did he do?"

"Neither, once he got over the shock. Things are going to be very interesting over at the newlyweds' house. I'd like to be a fly on the wall."

"Shame on you."

"Only long enough to hear what they say to each other. For a king's daughter, you do have a nasty mind." He glanced at me with a roguish gleam in his eye. I could almost hear the question trembling on his lips—if it wasn't his skill I had qualms about, what was it? But apparently he decided that even the question would be a contravention of his promise. "Believe I'll turn in," he said instead. "It's been a hard day. Good night." These rooms had no connecting doorway, and he went back out into the hall to go to his room.

It was as well he hadn't asked his question, I mused as I got ready for bed. Because I didn't have an answer. My first sight of him, charging down that bloody hall at me, foam on his lips and claymore swinging, had certainly not been a reassuring one. On the other hand, I probably hadn't looked especially attractive either. His initial advances had been too abrupt and much too soon, and I had taken offense at the fact that he had misinterpreted my medical ministrations.

He was an attractive enough man, once you got used to the larger scale. His face was always pleasant, and when he was dressed and combed and shaved, he was magnificent. His great size and strength in another man might have given me pause, for if he had been inclined to roughness he could have inadvertently done a lot of damage. But I knew him better now, and I would have cheerfully staked my life that he would prove to be a gentle and considerate lover. Nor could I doubt (remembering the feel of his fingers on the nape of my neck) that the feminine in me responded to the masculine in him.

It would please him, too, if I took him for a lover. This was no small consideration. I wouldn't accept a man who came to my bed driven only by his physical urges, a man for whom any woman would do. Nor yet would I accept one who came reluctantly, only to please me. Huard would value me for myself.

But! But I had gotten into the habit of defending myself from him. But he might think I came to him only from gratitude for the gifts he gave me. But I might suspect myself of using my body to keep him by me—unworthy thought! Surely I wasn't so much a whore as that—or was I? There was only one way to prove that to myself beyond all doubt, and that was to refuse myself to him and bid him farewell cheerfully when he left, as he was sure to do.

One thing was certain. I couldn't ask him to button the blouses he had bought me. On that dismal thought, I fell asleep.

Chapter Five

✥ ✥ ✥

"Eldrie, boars are dangerous. And from the tracks, this is the biggest one I've ever seen. I don't mean any insult to your courage or your skill with weapons, but I don't want you with me. It isn't safe."

"Huard," I mimicked, "boars are dangerous. No one in his right mind goes after one alone, without even dogs to draw it off if he goes down. And I'm all the huntsman you've got. And furthermore, if you think I'm going to sit in this inn and worry about you all day, you can just think again. Someone has to be there to tuck your guts back in and sew you up after the beast disembowels you."

He looked at me and his jaw set stubbornly. "And who sews you up? I'm no hand with a needle."

"I have no intention of getting close enough

to the beast to be endangered. Surely you've been hunting with me often enough to know that I know how to stay out of the way. And before you give me that order I can see on your lips, I want to remind you that you swore to obey me. Not the other way around. I'm ordering you to let me go with you."

"Eldrie," he began dangerously.

"Look, Huard, we can argue all day about it, and you never will get after the boar. Or you can just leave and I can follow you. But you can't stop me from coming."

He threw up his hands. "All right. Stay out of my way, and if you get killed, I'll—I'll—I'll never forgive you!"

I giggled, and his angry glare softened into a reluctant grin. "I won't mind having a little backup, I guess," he admitted. "There isn't anyone in the world I'd rather have backing me, either. But, Eldrie, honestly, you aren't big enough for boar hunting. It takes beef as well as courage to hold a boar on the end of a spear."

"I know," I said. "I've been on boar hunts before. But we always had dogs and archers to protect the spear handlers. I'm frightened for you, Huard."

"I'm flattered. Come on, let's go."

We had seen the damage the boar had done— indeed, the folk of Granton could have paid us three times what they had offered and still have been ahead by the end of the summer. As sometimes happens with an old rogue, this boar made a habit of destroying what he couldn't eat. His tracks were as big around as soup bowls and there was a rank smell in the air that lingered around the wheat fields where he had been. The mere thought of attacking him made

my skin crawl; I wanted to beg Huard to leave
the monster alone. I had better sense than to do
that, of course. I picked up my boar spear and
followed him out of the inn.

"Surely you aren't taking your wife with
you!" exclaimed the spokesman of the delegation. A sizable crowd was watching us leave.

"My wife isn't like these swooning useless females of yours," Huard said coolly. "She's my
partner and my companion, as well as a skilled
healer and a formidable warrior in her own
right. You treat your women like children and
they behave like children. Serves you right." He
was nervous too, I realized; he never would have
spoken with such brutal directness if he hadn't
been on edge.

Offended, the man fell back. "She's your wife,
of course," he sneered. "I wouldn't care to risk
mine in such a dangerous business."

Huard colored. "Gentlemen," I said, interrupting what could have become a heated con-
frontation. "There's work to be done." All eyes
swiveled to me with that astonishment that the
men of Termontaine showed whenever a woman
spoke up.

Huard shouldered his spear and held out his
hand, and I put mine into it. We walked out of
the village hand in hand to the accompaniment
of a chorus of shocked whispers.

The forest that cloaked the Wilderness Range
was old and wild and tangled with trees and
deadwood and brambles. The boar had long
been unchallenged lord of his range and was
arrogant; his trace had worn a path that was
easy to follow, wending among the rocks and
trees. Huard's consummate woodsmanship allowed him to move through the mossy trunks

with comparative ease, and I was learning—I would never be his equal, but I was far more at home in the wild than I had been. I stayed just the right distance behind him so that I could protect his back and yet not interfere with his weapon. And it was I who first sensed the boar. "Huard," I mouthed, "smell the air."

He paused and raised his head, sampling the vagrant currents that had brought me the merest whiff of the boar's rank odor. Reaching back, he handed me his spear, and I held it at his side where he could snatch it with a movement of his wrist. He strung his bow and nocked a heavy arrow. Then we waited. The boar didn't know we were here yet. When he did, he wouldn't flee, he would attack. We were intruders in his domain.

The air currents shifted, stirring the tendrils of hair on my forehead. Huard was concentrating on the thicket ahead; I kept glancing at all the coverts about. The boar might well sneak around to attack on the flank; it wouldn't be the first time a crafty old rogue had done so.

There was a querulous grunting. The boar had caught our scent. Huard drew the bow as far as it would go. With a squeal of rage, the boar broke cover, tail standing stiff and straight, red eyes gleaming. The bow sang; the arrow buried itself to the feathers in the massive chest, and the beast charged, tusks swinging.

Huard seized his spear from my hand and braced himself to meet the raging charge of a creature that weighed as much as one of my ponies. I dropped my own spear-point into line, shying out to the right so as to catch the boar under the foreleg and hopefully penetrate to the heart, while Huard held him upon his point.

Faster than a galloping horse, the foaming beast came down upon us, not at all inconvenienced by a yard of metal-tipped arrow in his body. Inches from the gleaming tip of the boar spear, he swerved, throwing foam in an arching spray, and lunged at me, squealing. Instinctively, I dropped the point of my spear and braced myself. With an impact that jolted me to the bone, he hurtled onto the spear-point. And then I was struggling to hold him, I instead of Huard with his great strength and weight. Blindly I clung to the shaft, knowing that if I lost my grip I was dead. I was flung about like a rag on the end of a whip, battered against tree boles and boulders as I scrabbled for a foothold. Over the pounding and the squealing I could hear Huard cursing as I had not known he could. Suddenly another spear sprouted from the boar's side, and as suddenly shattered. I was screaming with fear and rage and even a sort of mad exaltation.

"Hold on, Eldrie! Hold on!" Huard bellowed as he towered above the boar's back, claymore raised high. There was a *chunk!* as of a butcher cutting meat with a cleaver, and the boar screamed in crescendo, spraying blood. My feet hit the ground again and I braced myself, staring into the mad red eyes. The beast's spine had been severed by that mighty blow; still he strove to climb up the spear and destroy me, pawing at the earth with his forefeet as he dragged his useless hindquarters.

Again Huard struck, and at last the doomed beast began to fail, convulsing as he sagged to the ground, dragging my spear-point down

with him. Even his dying convulsions were
enough to fling me about, and I clung doggedly
to the haft of the spear in spite of the blood-
slipperiness of the thing. The red eyes glazed.
The boar was dead.

The reeling universe settled back into place,
sky above and ground below. I stared down at
the defeated enemy that had so nearly been the
end of me.

"Eldrie, you can let go of the spear now. Eldrie?" I stared stupidly down at the boar. I
heard Huard's words and understood them, but
they conveyed no impetus to action. Big hands
covered mine and began to pry them loose. "Let
go, Eldrie, let me look and see where you're
hurt."

With a tremendous effort, I dragged my attention back to Huard. "I'm not hurt," I said
thickly. "Are you hurt?"

"I'm fine, Eldrie, but you aren't. You're all
over blood. Let go of the spear, please."

I dared not let go. I was beginning to tremble
with shock and reaction. If I had let go, I would
have fallen in a heap at Huard's feet, and after
I had forced myself upon him, that would have
been a crushing humiliation. "You were right,
I'm not big enough to hunt boar," I chattered
between clenched teeth.

"Hell and damnation, you couldn't have done
better if you'd been three times the size," he
said. "Oh, Eldrie, if you ever scare me like that
again, I'll—I'll—here, let go the spear. Hold
onto me."

"I can't, I'll fall."

"I won't let you fall. Look, I've got you. Let
go. You can't hold onto it forever."

At last my trembling eased enough so that I

could, finger by finger, release my death grip on the spear, leaving bloody handprints behind. And Huard did keep me from falling, scooping me up into his arms and carrying me away from the rank stench of the boar's carcass.

"I can walk," I lied indignantly.

"From here to the ocean, no doubt," Huard agreed, but he didn't put me down. I put my numb arms around his neck and let my head fall on his shoulder.

Presently he laid me down on a grassy bank, and I was glad enough to stretch out and close my eyes. I was beginning to feel ill, and the pain of my numerous bruises and scrapes flooded in from every limb. Inch by inch, Huard examined me, running his hands over each arm and leg and down my ribs, searching for broken bones. In spite of the tenderness of my macerated skin, it was not an unpleasant process.

"Nothing broken, as far as I can tell," he said, sitting back with a sigh.

"I told you."

"You also told me you weren't hurt. You look like raw meat."

"Most of the blood is the boar's. I've got a bump or two," I said, struggling to sit up. Huard caught me around the shoulders to support me. "Just let me rest a minute and wash up and I'll be fine." In actual fact, I was better than I looked; I had escaped all but the most superficial injuries. I was malingering, enjoying the attention and concern Huard was lavishing on me, and I was ashamed of myself. "How about you?"

"I'm in a bad way, myself," Huard said with a grin. "That damn boar stepped on my toe. And I was hit with a flying princess two or three times, but that wasn't so bad; princesses are soft."

I rested for a few more moments. Then Huard built a fire while I wobbled down to the stream that ran a few yards away and washed off the blood as best I could. I made us each a cup of hot tea. Much restored, we set out for the village. There I went gratefully to bed while Huard took the delegation back to the site of the kill with a pack horse. The boar's meat would be too tough and rank to be edible, but they wanted to bring the carcass in anyway.

"Eldrie, supper's ready." Huard was bending over me, hand on my shoulder. "They're putting on a party for us. Can't you get dressed and come?"

I stretched luxuriously. "All right," I said lazily. "I'll wear the red brocade."

"Good for you! I'll go on down and stall them. Take your time." He was dressed in the blue outfit that became him so well; the belt with the silver buckle was around his middle.

Say what you like about the dour people of Termontaine, I mused, splashing briskly, their bathrooms were incomparable. In this country inn, Huard and I had to share a bathroom, but still there was hot water waiting to pour out of a tap. I would have to find out how they did it and have one installed in my own home, if I ever had one. My hands were a little swollen, but I flexed them vigorously and managed to dress myself. I even figured out how to fasten the clasp on my pectoral—no, Huard's pectoral, I reminded myself. I used a bit more of the rouge this time—the vivid color and daring cut of the dress seemed to call for it. I even rubbed some lotion on my wrists and throat—it was intended for insect bites and poison ivy, but it smelled pleasantly spicy.

I came downstairs and turned into the taproom. There was a scent of flowers and the light of many lamps—the folk of Granton had been busy while I slumbered the afternoon away. There had been a jocular remark on my lips to the effect that I was starving, but the sudden silence of the crowd in the taproom as I came through the door prevented me from saying anything. I paused in the doorway as all the staring faces turned toward me.

Wearing the heeled slippers, I was taller than anyone in the room, except of course for Huard. He turned and saw me. For a moment he stood and stared and I wondered if he recognized me. He hurried through the motionless people toward me, but when he came within a few steps, he stopped suddenly and made me a sweeping and graceful bow. As I had seen my father and the queen do a thousand times in like circumstances, I inclined my head graciously and extended my hand to him. Taking it, he went down on one knee before me and kissed it. Then he rose and bowed again, indicating the way to the laden tables and remaining down until I passed.

The people of Granton, who had never seen royalty before in their lives, parted before me, and as I walked with stately grace down the aisle they formed, they bowed or made a curtsy according to their sex. I nodded with regal condescension, smiling first to one side and then the other. Oh, I knew how to play a royal part! I was as much entrapped by this ceremony as if I had been dragged in chains the whole distance.

I went to the head of the table as if by right.

A storm of cheering broke out, and under the cover of noise, still smiling, I hissed to Huard, who had followed at my elbow (correctly, if I had been what I was being forced to pretend to be), "What have you been telling these people about me?"

"Just how you killed the boar." There was no time for more; the cheers were dying away and the townsfolk were gathering to stand behind their places. I waited until I was sure everyone was ready, and then I sat down. In a wave of subdued chatter, the people sat down too. Waiters began scurrying forth from the kitchens with the food, and bowing awkwardly as they presented it to me first; I waited with lofty patience while Huard served me. Everyone watched me to be sure that they didn't begin to eat before I did.

There was a man sitting on my left (Huard had been placed at my right) who was obviously a man of some standing in the community. Timidly, he spoke to me. "Er—Your Majesty . . ."

I glanced at him, the tiniest of frowns between my brows. "Princess Eldrie is correctly addressed as 'Your Highness,' " Huard informed him kindly and mendaciously, as I had no vestige of a right to either title. "Eldrie Fitzroi" was my proper styling, but I wasn't about to correct the misapprehension.

"I beg your pardon, Your Highness. We're just a little country town and we don't often entertain persons of your rank. Indeed, we've never had royalty here before."

"I understand completely," I said kindly. "In fact, I'm not here on state business. I'm traveling incognito, and I hope you'll treat me just like any other visitor."

"Oh, yes, of course, Your Highness. If you'll forgive us for any lapses in propriety."

I graciously agreed. It was a stiff and uncomfortable meal. I had heard that those who have no royalty of their own were much more profoundly impressed than those to whom a king was just another official, and if these people were any indication, it was true. I also knew from my own observation that true royalty tolerated rather than sought adulation, and I was rapidly finding out why—it was boring. Perhaps the measure of royalty is the gracious toleration of boredom, I reflected ruefully.

When the meal was over, I moved about the room, speaking kindly to the people, especially the women, who blushed and stammered and memorized my every word. They had a wonderful time. I withdrew just before the evening became too long for them, thus freeing them to go home and marvel. Huard attended me with grave propriety.

I turned to him when we got up to our rooms. "Huard, what possessed you to tell those poor people that I was a princess?"

"I didn't," he said defensively. "I told them how you killed the boar. Then you appeared in the door and stopped there. You looked so grand and beautiful and queenly that I couldn't help myself—I bowed to you. It was you that came walking into the room like you were conferring a blessing on us just by breathing the same air." He smiled at me. "Eldrie, I wish you could have seen yourself then. No one could have doubted for an instant that you were a king's daughter. I didn't have to tell them. They knew. And it was you who showed them."

I stood and looked at him sternly. "Huard, I

may be a king's daughter. But I am not a princess. And furthermore, I didn't kill the boar.
You did, and saved my life into the bargain."

He bowed low to me, and, taking my hand
and kneeling before me, kissed it. Looking up
at me with a mischievous smile, he said, "But
just think what a thrill you gave those people.
All the rest of their dull little lives, they'll be
talking about the princess who came and killed
the boar and ate dinner with them. They'll tell
their grandchildren how kind and gracious she
was, and how beautiful and brave."

I laughed. "Oh, Huard. Get up and don't talk
nonsense."

He rose, still chuckling. "Shall I unfasten the
pectoral for you before I go to bed?"

Now, I had put the thing on by myself, and I
was certainly capable of taking it off. Also, I
had very sensibly decided not to let Huard
touch me unless it was absolutely necessary.
But I meekly turned my back on him and let
him unfasten it, which he did with commenda-
ble dispatch. Even so, his breathing quickened,
and he thrust the pectoral at me and turned
hastily toward the connecting doorway between our rooms. "Huard," I said softly, and he
stopped abruptly. "Er—thank you for saving me
from the boar."

"You're welcome." He hesitated. "Eldrie . . ."

"Yes?" I answered quickly.

He hesitated again, then shook his head.
"Good night."

"Good night." He went on through the opening, and I'm sure he wished that there was a
door in the frame so that he could have closed
it with firm finality.

I stood in the middle of the floor, looking at

the pectoral that draped over my hand in liquid profusion. It was I who had made this silence between us. I was as sure as a woman can be that he had wanted to stay with me tonight, that he had almost spoken the words. I had wanted him to stay (I remembered his hands touching me as he searched for broken bones). Yet so well had I schooled him that he hadn't dared to speak. How was I to let him know that my feelings were changing, that now I might—no, I would—welcome his embraces?

I took the box out and piece by piece laid the jewelry in the proper places. There was no action I could take, no words I could say. My rejection had been too final. Yet I had lain there blissfully enjoying his touch as he searched for broken bones. I excoriated myself as a hypocrite. Come to think of it, I was amazed that anyone could feel any desire for such as I. Maybe I had misread his feelings.

I took a shaky breath. No, I hadn't, nor mine either. It had taken me a time to come to it, but I wanted him as much as he wanted me. There was only one thing to do, and that was to make the offer myself. The idea quite took my breath away; I hadn't been anywhere near as frightened when I found myself facing the charging boar.

Fingers trembling, I took off the brocade dress. Going into the bathroom, I washed, preparing myself for bed as I always did. Then I went to my medicine bag and took out a certain jar. I made myself ready so that if he accepted my offer, I wouldn't become pregnant.

I hesitated, thinking. I didn't quite have the courage to undress completely. Anyway, if he accepted, I wanted it to be because he wanted

me, not because he was overwhelmed by his
own masculine nature. He had to have the op-
tion to refuse, if he wished, as I had. And if he
did refuse, it would certainly be no more than
I deserved.

I was wearing a linen shift, a soft, shapeless
garment. That would do. I took a step toward
the connecting door, only to halt, paralyzed by
nervousness. This wasn't the right night, I told
myself cravenly. I had slept all afternoon, but
Huard would be tired. He was no doubt already
asleep, and wouldn't thank me for waking him.
Tomorrow would be better. We'd be away from
the oppressive effect of these sour-faced people
and camping under the stars. Or the next night.
Perhaps I should wait awhile and let the memory of my rejection of him grow dimmer. It
would give me a chance to be sure of my feelings. I took a step toward my own bed.

No, I told myself fiercely, beating down the
panic. Do it now! Get it over with! Surely he'll
turn you down—what normal human could pass
up an opportunity for so sweet a revenge? And
then it will be over and done. Clenching my
fists, I turned and took a step toward the door.
Come on, I exhorted myself silently. All he can
do is say no, and that won't be fatal. I took another step.

But what if he says yes? I asked myself. And
sometime down the future path, when we have
a quarrel, he points out in anger that it was I
who came importunate to him? What could I
say then? Oh, no, I couldn't face that. Surely
there was some way I could hint subtly to him
that his advances would be welcomed. In a few
days, I might remark on how silly I had been to
object to riding with him. Maybe sometime later

when I was riding with him, I could nestle trustingly into his arms and look wistfully up into his face and sigh. I could ask him to button up a blouse—or better yet, unbutton one. I retreated toward the bed.

I shook myself in a sudden fit of self-loathing. What a coward I was! He had been brave enough to risk rejection, and been brutally humiliated for his pains. Surely I could take three steps to the door and at least see if he were asleep. If he were, I wouldn't bother him. That wouldn't be right. The poor man needed his rest. This resolution carried me as far as the door frame, where I clung, panting as if I had run a mile.

There was quite a bit of light spilling through the door from my room, but I could see nothing but a heap of bedclothes. I listened. There was no sound, not even the regular, heavy breathing of sleep. But then, Huard didn't snore. If he were awake, wouldn't he have asked who was there? No, he was probably asleep, and if I crept away very quietly, he'd never even know I had been there. Emboldened by this thought, I whispered very, very softly—hardly a breath— "Huard, are you asleep?"

"No."

I jumped and clutched at the door frame. He wasn't asleep—I had never heard anyone utter a monosyllable that sounded less asleep—and worse yet, he knew I was there. Well, there was nothing for it now but to go through with it. With some of the fatalistic resignation of the criminal mounting the scaffold, I walked across the floor and slipped into Huard's bed.

For a moment he was still, and then he raised himself on his elbow and looked down at me.

"Eldrie," he said awfully, "you aren't teasing me, are you?"

I caught my breath. "Huard, if I were teasing, I would certainly deserve anything that happened to me, up to and including strangulation, wouldn't I?" Tentatively, I reached out and touched his lips very lightly with the tips of my fingers. "Perhaps I should make myself clearer. Huard, would you please make love to me? I ask it of you knowing perfectly well that I deserve to be dumped out of this bed and sent back to my own room. But would you, please?"

He laughed, a little breathlessly. "I wouldn't worry about being dumped out if I were you. But, Eldrie, are you sure? Before it's too late, are you sure? I'm only a simple hunter from a family of commoners. Are you really sure you want this?"

I moved closer to him and laid my cheek against his bare chest, feeling the restrained passion of him in the barely perceptible shivers that coursed through his skin. "Huard, my dear, will you make me beg?"

"No, Eldrie, never." With a great shuddering sigh, as of a wild and unbroken stallion at last surrendering to bridle and bit, he gathered me into his arms.

I had been right. He was patient and considerate. He wanted nothing unusual, but he made very sure not to rush me. And he talked. He told me what he was going to do, and what he liked me to do for him. He let me know what he felt, and when I tried shyly to tell him what I wanted him to do and what I felt, he listened and responded. It was, beyond anything I had ever experienced, sweet and joyous.

Twice during the night I was wakened with

soft kisses and a searching touch. "You must have been long deprived indeed," I said with a drowsy chuckle after the second time.

"Oh, yes, a very long time," he said. "I'm not one to lie with a woman I don't like, nor force myself on the unwilling."

There was a faint gray light stealing into the room from outside. "No," I said, "I wouldn't have suspected that of you. But it's a shame."

He propped himself on his elbow and smiled down upon me. "What is?"

"That you're so sparing of yourself. The rest of the women of the world don't know what a treat they're missing."

"They'll have to suffer. Ah! Would you, then? Princesses don't play fair, do they? There, how do you like that?"

I gasped. "Oh! No, Huard, I was only teasing. Good heavens, man, are you insatiable? Please! I cry mercy."

"Well, then," he said indulgently, "kiss me sweetly, and I'll let you off. For now."

So I kissed him as sweetly as I knew how, and received as good as I gave. "Huard," I said, presently.

"Yes, my sweet?"

"I don't think I want to hunt for a home."

"What do you want to do?"

I took a deep breath. "I want to find a healing mage. A spell doctor."

"What for?"

"I want to learn how to heal with magic. There's so little I can do with my herbs and balms. If I had known magic, I could have saved that little boy. And there have been others I couldn't save, lots of them."

He gave me a troubled look. "There must be

some reason why there are so few spell doctors, Eldrie. Either it's very difficult and dangerous to learn, or the magical healers don't take students. Or perhaps you have to have some special inborn talent to become a healing mage."

"Perhaps. But I'd like to try. For any physician, life is a long learning process. You strive and struggle to learn more so you can save more patients. In the end, no one learns enough. But you have to keep trying."

"I think you should go home," he said bluntly.

"I haven't got a home."

"Yes, you do. You should go back to your father. Eldrie, you are royal. I don't care whether your mother was wed to your father or not. I saw you down there last night, and you are not like other people. Aren't kings supposed to be given greater-than-common gifts and greater-than-common burdens?"

"Nonsense. Kings are just people. They don't have any special gifts. And even if they did, I wouldn't have any of them. I'm just an itinerant healer."

He shook his head. "No, you aren't just a healer. You are royal. Those people felt it as much as I did. They never bowed down in all their lives to anyone, but they bowed down to you. You have the gifts, all right."

"I'm just like anyone else. You should know. Am I any different from any other woman you ever lay with?"

"Yes. Oh, not physically. Yours is a deliciously female body, meant to give pleasure and to be pleasured. But there is a—I don't know, an invisible glow about you. Last night was like—well, lying with a being from another world, a better world. Oh, I'm not eloquent enough to say what I mean."

"But, Huard, I felt that too, and you say you're not of royal birth."

"I'm not. Just an ordinary, common family. Being with you lent me a grace, a glory, that doesn't belong to me; that must be one of the royal gifts, that you can imbue those around with a power they don't have of themselves. You must go home, Eldrie, they need you there. Your father needs you. You have the royal gifts, but you've run out on the royal burdens."

"Huard, they don't need me. I was never more than an inconvenience and a problem to them. I've been gone for sixteen years and I've never hidden. If they needed me so badly, why did they never send so much as a letter to ask me to come back?"

"I don't know, Eldrie. I only feel with all my being that you must go home."

I sat up, pettishly drawing the covers about me. "That's mystical nonsense. Royal people are only people, with only ordinary powers. And other people haven't got any business having premonitions about them. I'm going to look for a magical healer, Huard. You can do as you like."

Gently he laid a hand on my shoulder and pulled me down again. "You're my princess, Eldrie. I'll go wherever you like and do as I am commanded. But you can't command me to think any differently than I do."

I snuggled next to him and let him wrap his long arms around me. "You have never, ever obeyed one single order I ever gave you," I grumbled. "I certainly wouldn't think of trying to command your thoughts."

"I always obey you, Eldrie—at least, I obey the *real* commands you give me."

"Then don't ever mention going home again. Don't call me a princess. And don't natter on about royal gifts and royal burdens."

He chuckled. "Those aren't real commands."

"Somehow, I thought not. Oh, well. How about this one? Let's get up and get some breakfast."

"Now that's an order I can follow with enthusiasm. I hear and obey, O Princess."

Chapter Six

✤ ✤ ✤

HUARD WAS WAITING with his horse and the loaded ponies when I came down from a final check of our rooms for forgotten items. He was talking to the innkeeper, and as I came into the street before the inn, I saw him give the man a folded paper. Turning away, he looped the ponies' lead through a ring on his saddle. With a graceful bow, he held out his hand to me, and the loitering people murmured with delight. He boosted me into his saddle and led the horse out of Granton, creating out of our simple departure a royal progress, while I sat there in my dull and worn shirt and trousers, nodding and smiling at the people who gathered to see us go. I felt ridiculous, but apparently the people were pleased, in spite of my lack of splendor, for they waved and smiled and cheered. I suppose they thought that princesses traveling incognito always wore shabby clothes.

Once we were clear of the town and out of sight, Huard mounted behind me, and I snuggled against him. "I forgot to collect our money," he said regretfully.

"How could a princess possibly accept a fee for protecting the people?" I asked severely. "She doesn't just present a bill; only lesser folk do that. Now, if I were really royal, I'd levy a tax, and it would cost them a lot more than a fee."

"You're right, of course," he sighed. "Asking for the money would have ruined the whole marvelous illusion. How are we going to find a magical healer?"

"We'll travel until we find someone and then we'll ask," I said. "Someone we meet will have heard of one, and we'll follow their directions and ask again."

"It sounds like a long journey we've got ahead. Why don't we start by going to your father's country?"

"Huard," I said warningly.

"Well, there's as much chance your people know something as anyone," he said in an injured tone.

"South. We're going south," I said, only because my homeland lay to the north.

"Very well," Huard conceded. "South it is."

As pleasant as it was to ride with Huard's arms about me, I walked much of that day. Whenever we came to a little village, Huard and I would inquire of the innkeeper about a healing mage. It seemed that my choice of directions had been an inspired one, for when those we asked did know of a rumor of a spell doctor, it was always to the south they pointed.

We skirted the mountains and the edge of the ancient forest all that day, and by the late afternoon, we had left the settled farming lands miles behind. I was walking along, enjoying the cooling of the day and thinking my own thoughts, while Huard put his big mount to a jarring trot and rode ahead to spy out a camping place for the night. I sauntered around a bend and found him sitting his horse at a fork in the road.

"I thought you might like to see this," he said as I came up to him. "Which way do you want to go?"

I looked down the southern road. It was dwindling, becoming rockier and more weed-grown as it led off to the south. I knew where it went. It led to the Protectorate, a dingy land inhabited by grasping merchants, who were taxed into near bankruptcy to support their Protector's ostentatiously lavish lifestyle. Anything at all could be purchased in the Protectorate, was their boast, and it was partly true—anything at all that was shoddy and tawdry could be purchased for twice its worth. The people of the Protectorate fancied themselves great rogues and rovers; in truth, they were merely sly and dishonest, and tramped about with their pack trains and goods wagons on well-traveled roads, striving to cheat whomever was unwary enough to buy from them. At this they doubtless would have been more successful were it not for their habit of boasting about their schemes to defraud the innocent. I had been there several times and was always glad to leave.

I turned and looked up the other road. It led into the forest, climbing gradually as far as I could see. Last year's leaves lay in a brown carpet, undisturbed since they had fallen and the rains of winter had packed them down. Yet it was a fair, broad highway, cleared of stumps and rocks, the overhanging limbs that might impede a horseman's progress neatly trimmed back. Such a road as this would be styled the King's Highway in any civilized land. I knew nothing of it; I had never seen it on any map I had studied. The tips of my fingers tingled as I thought of the wide and easy road that led to the country of the little folk of legend. Or the story of how the ogres made it convenient for weary travelers to come to their banquet halls, there to serve as the main course at the feast. I had been much addicted to fairy tales—gruesome ones—as a child.

"I don't know this road," I said at last to Huard (not mentioning my lurid imaginings). "Do you?"

"I didn't even know it was here. What lies in that direction?"

"More mountains, I think," I said doubtfully. "I wonder who built it and why?"

"It sure is a better road than the one south to the Protectorate," he said wistfully.

"I'll tell you what, Huard, I know there aren't any mages in the Protectorate. And if we got any information there, we'd have to buy it."

"Only to discover it was a complete fabrication," he agreed. "Shall we ride along this road for a while, just to see where it goes? We can always come back to the Protectorate later."

I smiled up at him. "If this were a fairy tale, those words would make it absolutely certain that we'd never see the Protectorate again. Or ever be heard from again, most likely."

He actually shivered. "Don't talk like that. Precognition is bound to be one of the king's gifts."

"Huard," I said with exasperation, "there are no such things as king's gifts. And if there were, I wouldn't have them. I have just as much right to talk nonsense as anyone."

He grinned at that and extended a hand down to lift me to the pommel of his saddle. "Sorry," he apologized. "It's just that occasionally it all overwhelms me. My lover is a king's daughter! I can hardly believe that it should have happened to such an ordinary fellow as me!"

I settled myself comfortably. "I could say just as easily that I can hardly believe that it happened to me, plain and unexciting as I am, that my lover is tall and handsome and kind and gentle and generous, a great hunter and a fierce warrior. And good at fastening things." I felt myself drawn back into an embrace, and raised my mouth to his sweet, seeking kisses.

After a time—we were out of sight of the fork in the road when at last I looked around—I asked him, "Come to think of it, why do you believe it? It's a pretty unlikely story on the face of it, and for every true daughter of a king roaming the world, there must be a thousand who claim the part falsely. No one else ever believed me."

"I expect that no one else ever looked up from flat on their back on the floor and saw you standing over them with a sword in your hand and stern justice in your face, as I did. And then I begged mercy, and somehow, by some infinitesimal margin, you found me worthy of it. I offered my oath, and you took it and granted me your protection. And when you accepted my oath, you accepted responsibility for me; nothing less occurred to you. Oh, I knew who you were—or at least what you were. And you trusted me—the oath was given and taken and you knew—knew!—I wouldn't harm you. I was your true liegeman from the moment you fell asleep in my arms." This had started out as a simple explanation, but by the end, his face was shining. It was no less than a declaration, and how could I fail to respond to it?

I sat up. "Huard," I said gravely, "if I were truly royal, and if I had you for a friend, I would count myself the most fortunate of rulers. And if I were the lowest peasant in the land, and had you for my lover, I would count myself the luckiest of women."

He was silent for a long time, while the big horse carried us soundlessly over the carpet of leaves and the ponies bobbed along after us. "Do you still claim not to be royal?" he said in shaken tones. "Eldrie, I am yours. Don't blind me with your glory, but remember that I'm only a poor hunter."

I sighed, but said nothing. To him, the simplest declarations of human friendship were beginning to take on a mystical power. He was putting an unbridgeable distance between us; soon the woman who only last night had moaned with pleasure in his arms would seem no longer human to him. And I, alone and in sore need of the kindness and companionship he could offer so abundantly to a merely human woman, would be even more alone. There was nothing I could say to make him understand that I didn't need his worship, I needed his friendship.

"I've disappointed you, haven't I?" he said, interrupting my reverie. "You look as if your heart would break. What did I say to make you look so sad and defeated?"

I leaned back against him and turned my face so my cheek lay against his shoulder. "Hold me, Huard. I need you," I whispered. "Laugh at me. Tease me. Play jokes on me. Don't value me so highly that you make me inhuman."

"I'll try," he said slowly. "I think I understand why you ran away. They put all the burdens and none of the privileges of your birth on you, didn't they? And I was trying to do the same thing. I'll try to treat you as if you were any other pretty girl I'd seduced and lured into running away with me. Be patient with me when I forget to be disrespectful, will you?"

We camped that night in the murmuring forest. The air was sweet with summer, and far away in the depths of the wood, the foxes were calling their vixens. In the morning, we continued on our way. We had been traveling for only a couple of hours when we began to see signs of human presence—long gone and ruinous, a few tumbled blocks overgrown with trees hundreds of years old, their roots buried deeply in the loam of decayed trees that were ancient when these mighty forest lords had sprouted. There was a strange feeling as of hidden eyes watching—not threatening, but we were under some uncanny observation. In itself, that was unnerving.

Beside the road, a bubbling spring had been built into a cracked and stained bowl of white quartz rock. Whitenose was thirsty, for he pricked his ears at the music of the water. Turning toward it, he pulled the lead rope out of its ring and went to investigate, his faithful follower Graylegs right behind him.

"Stay here," I hissed to Huard. "Make no sudden moves." I slid down from the horse's back and went to retrieve the straying ponies.

Whitenose was feeling good. He was well-fed and lightly loaded, and he had always had a mischievous streak in him. Ninety-nine times out of a hundred, I could have walked up and picked up the lead rope and he would have made no objection. But not today. Quick as a cat, he twitched the rope out of my reach and sidled away.

Crooning endearments, I eased toward the pony again. One ear cocked toward me, he moved away just exactly fast enough to keep out of my reach. Graylegs's rope pulled out of its ring on Whitenose's pack, and he stopped and looked about in bewilderment, as if asking someone to please explain the joke to him. I picked up the rope and took him to Huard, who was, as I had asked, sitting still on the horse's back. I handed the rope up to him.

Whitenose was eating a flowering bush, one eye skinned back to be sure that I wasn't getting close enough to grab his rope. He watched me maneuver with amused interest; when I was nearly in position, he kicked up his heels and darted past me up one of the strangely regular aisles that led off the road.

There was nothing for it but to follow him. I trudged after him, following the neat small hoofprints around incongruously square corners and past inexplicably cubical mounds, some higher than hills. I hadn't gone twenty

yards when I realized that I could no longer see
Huard; I hastened on, hoping to catch the pony
quickly and get out of this labyrinth. I stepped
past a thick grove of saplings and found a re-
sentful Whitenose being held by a man dressed
in mottled gray and brown. His skin was
tanned, his hair was brindled gray and brown.
He was no taller than I and a little slenderer,
but his body was almost waistless. Indeed, he
was so like the tree trunks among which he
stood that for a moment I thought Whitenose
had caught his rope in a branch.

My step faltered, for the man was looking at
me with no welcome at all in his light brown
eyes. Then I said, softly, for this was a place of
silence, "Thank you for catching my pony. I
humbly apologize for intruding here and beg
that if any damage has been done, you allow me
to make it right."

The man handed me the lead rope and vanished. He did not duck into the brush; he did
not step aside or walk away. He vanished with
the abruptness of a popping soap bubble. The
hair on my arms stood away from my skin and
tingled as I coiled up Whitenose's lead rope and
hastened down the trail.

I was appalled to find Huard, dead or unconscious, draped over the saddle, face down. I had
left him sitting his horse normally; I had been
gone no more than fifteen minutes. I had heard
no disturbance. What could have happened to
him? Was I about to be struck down by the
same mysterious agent?

I was not, nor was Huard dead. It seemed as
if he were slumbering, but no amount of shaking or shouting brought any response, and I
didn't want to pull him off the horse's back—I

never would have been able to get him back on and we had definitely been given notice to leave.

I scrambled up on the horse's back. It was a good thing the beast was docile, for it was a far climb without Huard to give me a leg up. Straddling the big gelding with Huard's body draped over the padded pommel in front of me, I kicked the horse into motion, and he started up willingly enough.

At first I was merely concerned with getting away from the vicinity of the gray men. The only way out of the clearing was the broad road upon which we had ridden into this forest; the direction the animals were pointed led us farther into the mountains, angling gradually to the southwest. For miles I rode through the almost obliterated remains of some metropolis more mighty than any in the known world. It was walled with twisted old trunks and whispering greenery, and canopied with the lofty, spreading crowns of the trees; if Whitenose hadn't strayed, I don't think I ever would have noticed the unnatural regularity of the jumbled heaps. I was not tempted to explore. It was not permitted.

I was worried about Huard, but as long as we were within the precincts of the ancient city, I dared not stop to examine him. We weren't unescorted. How did I know the followers were there? Not by sight, sound, or smell. Only by the actions of the birds and animals, by Whitenose's occasional snuffling of the air, by the prickling in the back of my neck, was I aware that in this vast forest there were presences other than our own.

As I rode, the old skills came back to me. As a girl, I had loved horses and I had ridden every

day after classroom lessons. Nor had I been the
sort of hoyden that was content to slop about
bareback, blissfully ignorant of the finer points
of the horseman's art. I had been determined to
learn from masters in every branch of riding
and driving, and in this I had been indulged by
my father's stablemaster. By the time I had left,
I had been a skilled horsewoman, wanting only
seasoning and practice to become a mistress of
the classical equestrian arts myself.

I had ridden very little since I had gone out
to make my own way in the world. The reasons
for this were many and complex. Only on horseback was I homesick, for on horseback my hap-
piest childhood hours had been spent. I had
never been able to afford a mount of the sensitivity of the animals that had been at my disposal in my father's stable, and it was sheer
torture to ride the sort of underbred, hard-
mouthed, jug-headed animal I could have purchased. But mainly, only on horseback did I feel
any vestige of my royal heritage. On horseback,
I was grand and high and important (in my
mind's eye), lent stature and impressiveness by
the horse that carried me. Speed and fear were
at my command, and the arrogance that I feared
I should have developed if I had been a princess
instead of a mere royal bastard lifted my chin
and squared my shoulders. No amount of reminding myself that I was the most ordinary of
commoners would slump me in my saddle or
allow my disdainful gaze to drop to earth.

So had my father always ridden—as if
mounted upon an imperial dragon rather than
a mere hay-eating horse. It was so I remembered him most fondly, riding in full royal pan-
oply in some ceremony or parade, the people

cheering and his gracious nods recognizing their homage first on one side and then the other. The harried, busy, always tired man who dealt daily with a tedious multitude of administrative decisions and a horde of petitioners was only my father, though I had been taught from my earliest memory not to bother him and so hardly knew him. The man on the horse was the king, whom I had loved with all my childish heart.

Perhaps my obsession with horsemanship had begun in a cherished hope that that splendid personage might recognize in that much a kinship between us, might someday call out to me to join him as he rode down the broad boulevard that led from the city gate to the palace. He never had, of course.

For a time then I had daydreamed of earning my father's gratitude by somehow saving the kingdom with my skill and daring on horseback. I had practiced vaulting on and off my galloping horse and weaving him through the most torturous tangles. I had also developed a passion for fencing, and my father's arms master had proven surprisingly willing to teach me. I had broken my collarbone falling off the horse and become a rather good swordswoman by the time cold reality intruded into my daydreams and I realized that if the kingdom had been threatened, I certainly shouldn't have been allowed to go dashing to the rescue.

The simple fact, I had finally had to realize, was that my brothers were right. I was useless and an embarrassment to my father, and he preferred to pretend that I didn't exist. There was nothing I could or should do to bring myself to his notice; he would simply have ar-

ranged to have me removed to a place where I
wouldn't pester him. For a time, I sought to find
a niche for myself about the palace, but although my birth wasn't high enough to entitle
me to any privileges, it was entirely too high
for me to be allowed to take up any useful occupation. So I left, nor had I ever regretted the
decision.

Except when I rode on horseback.

I emerged from my reverie to discover that I
was finding it very difficult to remember from
what we were fleeing. There were wisps of
memories—Whitenose had escaped and run
into the dark and we mustn't go there—no, that
wasn't right—but what was right? I rubbed my
forehead vigorously and managed to conjure up
mental pictures of trees and ruins of buildings
and men that were also trees, but they were
jumbled and confused.

I was far enough up the road that I might
stop and tend to Huard. Pulling up the horse
and dismounting, I eased him off the saddle and
down to the ground. Upon examining him, I
found no sign of injury, and I concluded that he
must have been heavily drugged or enspelled. I
could only wait and hope for his eventual re-
covery, and care for him in the meantime. I set
up camp near a small stream just on the edge
of the road. It seemed to me that as long as we
had stayed on the road, we had been safe,
though I couldn't quite think from what.

Whatever had been used on Huard, it was
powerful. It was nearly sunset before he awoke.
I was gathering wood on the edge of the forest
when I heard a sudden and desperate shout,
"Eldrie!"

I hastened back. Huard had wakened. Not

seeing me, he'd been understandably worried that something had happened to me. Or so I thought until I came within reach of his long arm. I was seized with crushing force around the wrist. "Eldrie! I thought you had run away," he said, wild-eyed as he glared up at me. "It won't do you any good if you do! I'll catch you."

"Ouch! Let go, you're hurting me. I wouldn't run away from you, Huard. Take it easy. I'm right here."

He shook his head as if clearing a mist from before his eyes. "Sorry," he muttered, shame-faced. "I was frightened. How did we get here? Why was I asleep?"

I rubbed my bruised wrist, eying him dubiously. He hadn't sounded frightened. He had sounded, and looked, threatening. "You were drugged," I told him. "I brought you here on the horse. We mustn't go back."

"Why not?"

"Because—" I rubbed my forehead. My head felt all full of cotton when I tried to remember what had happened. "Because the people—the forest— It isn't safe."

"What people?"

I could only shake my head. "I don't know," I said. "Don't you remember?"

"The last thing I remember before this camp was kissing you while we rode up a beautiful road."

It was too late in the day to move on, so we spent the night there. In the morning, we rode on. The forest was full of summer, life spring-ing exuberantly from the very earth. There was plenty of game and plant foods, and we used our supplies very sparingly. Medicinal plants abounded, and as we traveled I gathered and dried and packaged and simmered and mixed, until the dependable Graylegs nearly disappeared under his bulky but not very weighty burden of teas, elixirs, ointments, salves, and washes. I was fully stocked with all the medicines that could be derived from a great hardwood forest.

The golden days of summer were gilded further by the company of my lover. I had had lovers before. If I liked a man, and if there was a spark of mutual attraction between us, I wanted him; and though I had to admit that I wasn't beautiful, often enough I had achieved my desire.

Although I had from time to time taken lovers, and sweet were the memories I cherished for each of them, I had never traveled with one before. All day we walked or rode through a wild and lovely land, the rich clean odors of the forest as subtly intoxicating as sparkling wine. We saw no one, and only the marvelous road reminded us of the presence of other human beings in the world.

The times we spent ahorse were times for touching and kissing and laughing at our folly, and when we walked, the soft loam of the forest floor was an ever-present bed cleanly sheeted with the fallen leaves of autumns past. If the mood overtook us, we might easily draw aside from the road, leaving the animals to graze upon the grass that lined the verge, and lie down together under the spreading regal canopy of some dignified oak.

I was always careful to excuse myself for a few moments to prepare for such occasions, however. I wanted no issue of these sweet interludes! Perhaps Huard, who was by his own lights an honorable man, would have stayed to help me raise our woods-colt. He might even have offered to marry me in order to legitimize the child. But I knew in my heart that however much I might enjoy Huard, and however deep and abiding the affection we might feel for each other, any permanent arrangement would soon become unbearably irksome for us both.

There was only one flaw to these beautiful days and idyllic nights. Huard was laboring under some tension. He became irritable if I were long out of his sight, and I often awakened in the night to find him clutching at me. He claimed that nightmares disturbed him, and I dosed him with a nervine of lemon balm and basil. But it disturbed me that the long story he told me to account for his nightmares was a lie. I hadn't known him well enough before we had become lovers to judge whether he told me the truth or not, but I had come to assume that he was being as honest and straightforward with me as I was with him. I had never caught him out in a lie before.

I forced myself to dismiss the matter from my mind; I didn't want to escape from him. We were going where I wanted to go, and when it became necessary for us to part company, there wouldn't be anything he could do to stop me, short of physical restraint. And there was no reason why he should wish to hold me against my will.

I was almost sorry when we realized that the road, which had been gently declining in altitude for some days of travel, was leaving the mountains and the forest and taking us into open country. This land became more and more arid day by day—almost mile by mile. By the time we reached the foothills and the end of the road, we were in the desert.

It was a land of blue distances and furnace heat, and the sweet rich smell of the forest was replaced by a spicy pungency that tickled the nose. We found it more comfortable to shade up for the middle of the day under some thin-foliaged desert tree (I collected a good supply of the gum from these trees, an important medical ingredient). Then in the invigorating cool of the evening we would travel on, sometimes until late at night. We would sleep for a few hours and then rise very early to travel on again until the heat became too oppressive.

Water was a constant worry, but this was a trader's wagon road and took that necessity into consideration. The route passed by enough little desert springs and streams that we were never seriously endangered, though we did get thirsty a time or two.

I found that I was coming to love that wild and secret desert. I liked the openness. The plants fascinated me and the animals charmed me. I especially loved the little shallow streams that meandered over sandy beds vast enough for mighty rivers; they were havens of life in a harsh and thorny land. Birds and animals abounded in the cottonwoods and willows that lined their banks, and every stretch of wet sand was a signature-book of visitors' tracks.

"Huard," I said dreamily, one hot afternoon as we lazed in the dense shade of a murmuring cottonwood, "I've found it."

"What?" he asked drowsily.

"Home. This is where I want to live."

He laughed. "Here? In this wilderness? We

traveled too late this morning. You've got heat stroke."

"No, I mean it. I like it here. I'd go up into the mountains for the summer and to collect herbs. But this is where I want to live."

"But, Eldrie, there aren't any people here. How would you make a living?"

"That does present a difficulty," I admitted. "But this road must go somewhere, mustn't it? There must be people there."

He rolled over and looked across at me (we didn't snuggle up too closely during our day-time rests—it was too hot). "Eldrie, don't set your heart on living here. You have to go home."

"This is home."

He sighed. "Will you go home and at least see if you're needed there before we settle down here? If you'll do that, I'll never mention it again."

"You don't have to settle down here," I pointed out.

"If you do, I have to. You're my princess and I'm your liegeman."

I forebore to argue. We'd see just how far his oath went when it came right down to it. "Nevertheless," I said firmly, "I'm not going home. I'd never get away again."

The road led us on into the desert, and we found that there were towns sited near the big desert rivers. These had substantial plantations of irrigated land round about and town walls of rammed earth. The people were friendly and hospitable. That they were in touch with the rest of the known world was easy to see from the contents of the market stalls, which contained goods from many nations. Each town had two or three comfortable little inns, too, the kind where the accommodations are simple and the host is anxious to please. His wife was usually the cook, and prided herself upon her tasty and wholesome food.

I liked these cheerful, musical people, and began to think seriously of settling down in one of their towns. But none was quite large enough to support a physician full-time, especially since the people were the healthiest I had ever come across, well but simply fed, used to the rigors of an outdoor life, clean in their habits and persons. Many healers would disagree, I knew, but I judged that their happy dispositions improved their resistance to disease. Frequently they sang as they worked, and when gangs of them labored, they sang elaborate harmonies. Everyone had a smile and a wave for any passerby. They often were to be seen, resting from their labors and admiring some beauty of nature, the antics of a calf or lamb, or the attractiveness of some flashing-eyed black-haired girl, or if they were women, a clean-limbed laughing youth.

Whatever the reasons, though there were always several cases of injuries and the infirmities of childhood or age to be looked at when we arrived in a town, there was little for me to do, and no hunting at all for Huard. The people were appalled at the thought that anyone would kill the wild animals, which they regarded more as universal pets than as a source of food and leather.

Then I made a discovery that drove all thoughts of making a home out of my head. At every inn and shop, I always asked about a healing mage. One day as we were arranging for a room, instead of the usual vaguely positive answer, the innkeeper said casually, "Oh, yes, there's Mennefer, of course. You will have heard of her, though."

"No," I said eagerly. "Does she live near here?"

He gestured at the red-rock badlands across the valley from the river. "Over there. I could draw you a map if you like; it's a little hard for strangers to find."

"Surely many people go to her."

"Oh, no, we don't like to bother her. She won't take any fees, and magical healing is terribly difficult. They never live long, healing mages don't."

Huard caught my eye significantly at this. I ignored him. "Does she take students?" I asked. I was trembling with the intensity of my need to know.

"Well, now, I don't know," the innkeeper said, rubbing his chin. "She's just young herself. You could ask her, though. We'd like to know that there was someone up there with her. Hers is a lonely life."

"Draw me that map and I'll go to her," I said. "If she'll take me, I'll stay on as a student as long as she'll have me."

"I'll have it ready for you in the morning," he promised, waving aside the tip I offered him for his precious information.

I found it difficult to sleep that night, twisting and turning so much that Huard, grumbling sleepily, got out of bed and spread his bedroll on the floor. "I'm sorry," I apologized. "Come on back. I'll lie still."

"I'd just as soon sleep with a snake," he growled. "I'll be fine down here. Good night."

I slipped out of the bed and into the bedroll

next to him. "Huard," I purred into his ear,
making sure that my warm breath tickled a little, "are you really so sleepy as that?"

"What did you have in mind?"

I showed him.

Chapter Seven
❖ ❖ ❖

THE MAP BENNEM the innkeeper gave us the next
morning was a beautiful thing, drawn so that
the landmarks seemed to jump out of the page
in three dimensions, distances and directions
clearly marked. There were even exquisite little
colored drawings of the plants and animals we
might see along the way. "This is beautiful!" I
exclaimed as I studied it. "Far too lovely to use
to find the way. It should be framed and hung
on the wall."

Bennem glowed with pleasure and took us
into his private parlor, where many maps hung
in simple frames. Some were maps of real
places, and some were imaginary. "I like maps,"
the innkeeper confessed with simple pride. "It
makes a place more real if it's mapped. And
even a place that never existed at all becomes
almost real if there's a map of it." He stood before the largest map, which showed the known
world. "Have you ever thought how small a part
of the world we really know?" he asked, touching the countries one by one. "We know this
short section of coast and the coastal range—
here's the patchwork of small countries along

the coast, from Lumbrel in the north, mostly in the fir forest, to Savannade in the south. We here in the desert are about at the western border of the known world. And north, west, and south of these—unknown lands. To the east, the sea, and beyond that, what?"

"I wish I really were royal," I exclaimed. "I'd bring you to Maritiene and give you a fleet of the stoutest ships. I'd recruit and train companies of the bravest explorers to go into the unknown world. And I'd give you the finest studio and workshop in the city where you could sit and make maps when they all came back to tell you where they'd been and what they'd seen."

He looked at me, his simple, homely face glowing. "I wish you were royal too," he said. "I'd come and I'd make you the best maps that have ever been made, and I'd train up youngsters so the work could go on when I was gone. And the maps—the maps would be the greatest wealth of your kingdom. With them, you could send out traders. You could make treaties with the great empires which must lie out there. You could find the sources of the First Civilization and discover all the magical secrets of the old tales."

"Do you see, Eldrie Fitzroi? Do you see now why you must go home?" Huard said, his voice deep and vibrating. "You are truly royal, and you have the royal gifts! Could anyone less inspire such a vision?"

The innkeeper looked at me, and the glow died out of his face to be replaced by mingled fear and awe. "Are you really royal? Forgive me, I allowed my enthusiasm to get the better of me. I'm not really a cartographer, I'm just a stupid innkeeper." Bowing, he backed out of the room in confusion and went fluttering off.

I rounded on Huard. "How dare you? That poor man—and you had to spoil it with your babbling. If I were royal, I'd have you flogged until you bled. How dare you!" I was so angry I was hissing like a cat.

Huard gave me a long hard stare. "How dare I speak the truth? How dare I not? Your father says that the most valuable member of his court is the man who dares to tell him when he's wrong. Well, you're wrong, Eldrie, and I'm telling you so. Flog me if you like—as soon as we get back to Maritiene."

My anger died. "I wouldn't have you flogged, Huard, even if I had the power, which I don't. And even if we were going home, which we aren't. But please, please don't talk like that in front of other people. That poor man! He was so proud of his beautiful maps, and now he'll be waiting and wondering and worrying whether some day he might not be called to Maritiene. He'll never be really happy with these again." I waved a hand at the exquisite cartographical creations around us.

"As soon as you get back, send for him. Give him the things you said you would. He'll deliver just what he promised. Remember it."

"*I am not going home!*" I stormed out of the inn, grabbed up the ponies' leads, and jerked them around, setting off down the road at such a pace that Huard had to trot his big horse to catch up with us.

"Come on, Eldrie. Don't be angry with me for telling the truth." Huard leaned down from the saddle and held out a hand to help me up. "I'll admit that I was wrong to talk in front of Bennem. It seemed like such a good opportunity to make you see how wrong-headed you're being. If you were to go home, you'd have the power to do the kinds of things you were talking about."

I took his hand and let him lift me onto the padded pommel. "That's where you're dead wrong, Huard. I wouldn't have any power to do anything at all, not even to conduct my own life as I see fit. You don't understand. I am the king's daughter and there are many, many things that I couldn't do for fear of shocking and upsetting my father's people. I couldn't, for example, set up a practice as a physician in Maritiene City.

"But on the other hand, I am a bastard. I have no rank or standing in my own right, not from my mother, who's the younger daughter of a petty merchant, nor from my father. My father could have arranged that I be given a rank and the duties and responsibilities that go with it, but he chose not to. There's only one use they could have for me. There might be some petty border lord, some half-bandit of a baron whose loyalty it would be convenient for my father to secure. No one with any real power, mind you; such as that couldn't be fobbed off with a bastard. But if there were someone insignificant enough to accept me, I might be married to him. It would secure his loyalty and save my father a little annoyance. And I might languish for the rest of my life in some verminous keep."

Huard listened to this outpouring of old bitterness with silent attention. "I'm sorry," he said at last. "I hadn't realized what might be asked of you. I thought that you were needed

for what you are, not as a pawn in some sleazy
power brokerage."

"That isn't the worst that could happen," I
said. "My father is a relatively young man, but
he won't be king forever. My older half-brother
will be king then—and both my brothers hate
me. If one of them was scolded by their tutor,
and neither of them were keen scholars, he
could always go and slap me around until I
cried mercy. Later, when they entered puberty,
they could revenge themselves on me for exist-
ing by pointing out to me in great detail how
ugly I was, how undesirable, how revolting to
any man with any finer feeling at all. They em-
barrassed and humiliated me every way they
could."

"Your father permitted this?"

"Who would tell him? And what would they
tell him? Imagine telling the king, 'Your Majesty, the princes are being mean to your bastard. They call her names and yesterday they
circulated a poem claiming that she had bullied
a stableboy into engaging in unnatural carnal
acts with her in the manure pile. Permit me to
quote it, Your Majesty.' "

"Children can be cruel. But surely your
brothers are grown men now."

"Surely they are. But my older brother was
eighteen when I left, and only the day before he
tripped me when I was going in to supper so
that I fell flat on my face in front of the Protector's ambassador."

"Do you hate your brothers, Eldrie?"

I considered. "No," I said at last. "I gave as
good as I got. Not the same kind of thing, of
course. But I was better at everything than either of them. I was quicker with my studies,

and I'm afraid I wasn't above showing my superior understanding off in circumstances that made them look like fools—even my older brother. I rode better, too, and I could touch either of them at will when we fenced together. About the only way they could best me was by ganging up on me. Their nasty little poem wasn't true, but I had done a little kissing and exploring with one of the stable lads and the younger prince caught us at it once. I guess you might say, if you were considering things from my brothers' point of view, that I was a poisonous brat, and I'm sure they heaved a sigh of heartfelt relief when I was found to be gone."

Huard chuckled. "I'll admit that I was having a little trouble visualizing you as a helpless victim."

"Never that. Huard, how did you know what my father says?"

"Eh?"

"Back at the inn, you said, 'Your father says that the best friend a king can have is one who isn't afraid to tell him when he's wrong.' That's right, I've heard him say it a hundred times. But how did you know?"

"Oh . . . I've visited in Maritiene. Everyone quotes the king's sayings. I'm from Nordron, though."

"I see." Nordron was far north and inland from Maritiene, and there was little commerce between the countries. The Nordrons were proud and difficult to deal with and their country was poor in resources that they might have sold to other nations. Besides, the most direct routes between our countries lay across the lands of Maritiene's hereditary enemy, Adamar, and through the Salifer, the great salt marsh, which was impassable when it wasn't frozen. I knew much less about them than I did about the other nations of the known world. I had never been to Nordron.

For a moment, I felt suspicious of Huard—probably because I had been talking about my brothers, a reminder of past deceptions. But then I dismissed the suspicion. What devious purpose might he have? Even if he had been in Maritiene City and heard my father with his own ears, he could hardly have been in the wartorn Republic looking for me. And why should he? There was no price on my head. But it made me uncomfortable that he had lied to me once again. I so much wanted to trust him!

The animals' iron-shod hooves rang like bells on the red sandstone of the badlands. Sculpted by water and polished by the wind, spires of ruddy stone rose on all sides like twisted statues wrought by some demented giant. There was no life in this wilderness of rock and windborne pattering sand. "Do you suppose the innkeeper sent us in here deliberately, and this Mennefer doesn't even exist?" Huard asked through cracked and bleeding lips.

"No," I said firmly. "We're right on the path he drew for us. He wouldn't have gone to all this trouble just to send us in here to die—any fabrication would have done." For three days we had trudged through the badlands. The furnace heat of the sun reflected off the jumble of rock all around us, roasting us in an eerie sunset glow all day. In that three days we had had only a few swallows of water. We had brought water with us, of course, but the animals had been suffering and I had insisted upon sharing our canteens with them.

"Let me see the map again," Huard requested, lurching to a halt. We were both walking to spare the horse, which had suffered the most of any of us. He had refused his grain this morning, and even my greedy ponies had only lipped at theirs. Huard's great size and lack of stamina was beginning to tell on him; he was gaunt and hollow-eyed and made every excuse to stop and rest. There was nothing I could do to help him, even though I was relatively fresh.

I took the map out of my medicine bag and handed it to him. He unfolded it and peered at it through eyes red-rimmed from the constant glare of the sun. He was a man of the misty north; this desert was hard on him, I thought sympathetically. I should have freed him from his oath and sent him on his way before I dragged him into this red-rock wilderness. "According to this," he said, "there are dragons here."

He pointed out the tiny, perfect drawing, and I took the map and tilted it to get a better light. It was a dragon, right enough, and the innkeeper had been right about the song dogs and the tiny sand deer. "You're right," I said. "Maybe there are dragons. Or maybe it's a decoration. Let's go see." I folded the map with tender care and tucked it back into my medicine bag as I started off again, towing the reluctant ponies behind me.

Presently Huard spoke again. "Look, there's the rock that looks like a ship under full sail. The trail turns here."

"So it does, and goes down an incline. We're nearly there. I hope there's water below. Oh . . ."

We had walked around the ship rock and were standing at the top of a nearly vertical cliff of polished sandstone. Hundreds of feet below, a narrow ribbon of sand led among jumbled boulders, disappearing to the right. The trail down the cliff was a foot wide and clung to the sheer rock wall as precariously as a spider web.

"We can't get down that," Huard protested.

"I don't think we have any choice," I said grimly. "There must be water at Mennefer's place. We know there isn't any water between here and the river. The animals would never make it back. Your horse is nearly done in, and the ponies aren't much better. We have to get down it."

Huard swallowed. "Eldrie, I'm scared of heights."

"You did fine back on the coastal range. This isn't nearly as high. We'll turn the ponies loose; they'll follow the horse down." I took the lead ropes off the halters and tucked them into the packs. "Give me your hand," I said with more confidence than I felt. "I'll lead the way."

He placed his hand in mine, and not without misgivings of my own, I stepped off the rim.

Once on the trail, we had to stride along briskly; the huge horse right behind us was slipping and sliding, his iron shoes striking off long trails of sparks. Huard clutched convulsively at my hand, but gamely he kept coming. I didn't look down; the sense of space and blue air was almost palpable. The wall beside us was close enough to touch with our fingers; the trail cupped slightly and the edge was a foot's width away. The cliff sloped just enough away from the trail that the ponies could manage their packs, though again and again I heard the scraping sound of canvas pack covers on rough sandstone. I winced when I heard it; if the abrasion wore away the last ropes, the pack would shift and surely precipitate the pony carrying it over the ledge into the blue airy space beyond.

There was one place that was really bad. Here a great bulge of harder stone swelled out of the cliff like the vast sail of some petrified ship, billowing in a timeless wind. The trail was only a scuffed line of scratches across this and sloped sharply toward the drop-off. Huard stopped and made a whimpering sound in his throat when he saw it, but I stepped out on it determinedly. There was no going back and it was as well to die quickly in a fall as slowly from thirst.

My heart hammered and my knees trembled as we struggled across it, and gravity seemed to curve our path inexorably toward the horrific fall. It was a race between our momentum crossing the slippery stone and the drag of the earth far below; by the slimmest of margins, we reached the trail on the far side. The animals came floundering after, wild-eyed and blowing in terror. They made it too, and we all stopped and leaned against the cliff face, chests heaving. I glanced at Huard. His eyes were closed and his nostrils pinched; he was as lathered with sweat as if he had run for miles.

"I'm glad you're with me, Huard," I panted. "I've never been so terrified in my life. But I'd never have brought you if I'd known about this."

As I'd intended, this brought him out of his daze of terror. "I'd never have let you come if I'd known about this, not if I'd had to tie you up and carry you away over my shoulder," he retorted.

I forebore to argue with him about this statement, but started out again. There was long and
long to go on this terrible trail and the afternoon was waning. Down we went, and down,
until the muscles in the back of my legs ached
and my knees wobbled with the strain of holding back. The trail switched back again and
again, dropping lower with every leg, and flights
of shallow steps appeared—not carved by man's
hand, I judged, but worn into the native rock
by the slow, patient forces of nature.

It was a surprise to me when I found that I
was walking on sand. I halted and looked
around. We were in deep shade at the bottom
of a narrow cleft; the air was thick and purple.
The horse stood, legs spread wide and head
drooping until his muzzle almost rested on the
sand. Graylegs lay down under his pack.
Huard's head was bowed on his chest, staring
unseeing at the sand beneath his feet.

"We made it! We're down!" I said jubilantly.

Slowly Huard raised his head and looked
around. "I hope you like it here," he said bitterly. "Because if that's the only way out, we're
going to spend the rest of our lives down here."

After mastering that vertiginous trail, it
should have been as safe strolling along the flat
sandy bottom of the canyon as sleeping snug in
our beds at home. Yet it was here that disaster
struck.

The sand wasn't easy walking; it slipped from
beneath our feet, further tiring our already
weary legs as we picked our way among the
fallen slabs of sandstone. The horse and Graylegs had to be coaxed along. But not Whitenose.
He looked to be the more delicate of the two
ponies, but those pipestem legs were sinewed

with iron. In all the years I had packed him, sometimes heavily, and led him for long weary miles, I had never known him to be truly tired. As so it was now. There was a sudden flash of movement in the sand practically under his feet and a six-foot sand-colored serpent darted into the rocks. Whitenose shied. One forehoof came down on a teetering slab of sandstone, which pivoted. The pony went down suddenly, his other feet scrabbling vainly for purchase in the shifting sand. The boulder, relieved of his weight, came crashing down, and I could clearly hear the ominous snap of breaking bone.

"Whitenose!" I cried in agony, and ran to him, dropping Graylegs's lead rope. Hearing my voice, Whitenose quit struggling and lay still, waiting trustfully for me to do something to relieve his pain. I had always helped him before; how could he doubt that I would do so now? The great, dark, anxious eyes fixed upon me. I laid a hand upon his halter, steadying him as Huard bent his powerful muscles to lifting the slab off the pony's leg. He heaved until his muscles cracked, and the sandstone rose, and wobbled, and plunged over, raising a shower of sand. I stripped off the pack and pack saddle, and freed of his burden, Whitenose lunged to his feet. Three of them. One slender foreleg he held trembling above the sand, touched its toe down, lifted it again, champing his jaws. Then he stood patiently waiting for me to work my miracle.

I knew—oh, I knew!—that there was only one miracle I could work for that faithful pony and that was to put him out of reach of suffering. But I knelt to feel the leg anyway. In the middle of that fine flat-boned cannon there was a feeling of roughness, an audible grating sound, and already the flesh around the area was beginning to swell. Whitenose bent his neck to thrust once, lightly, at my shoulder with his muzzle, protesting the pain I was causing him. I crouched there in the dust, hiding the tears that started from my eyes and ran burning down my face.

He was only a pony—an old, used-up pony, at that. He had been marked as not very valuable from birth by his gray color. For the last year or so he had been troubled with wind puffs and I suspected he might have a ring bone starting in his off fore. But for all his faults, he had been my faithful companion and servant for fifteen years. I had no human friend who would have stood by me half so long.

"Eldrie." Huard's voice was gentler than I had ever heard it, as his big hands grasped my shoulders. "Eldrie, take the other pony and the horse on down the canyon. I'll take care of him."

I shook my head, unable to speak. I meant to convey that I would do what was necessary myself, but Huard misunderstood.

"You can't help him, can you? He can't move from here and we can't stay with him. And he's in pain, Eldrie. He doesn't understand. Let me put him down. I'll do it quickly and gently, I promise."

"No," I choked. "He was my friend. I'll do it."

The hands closed about my shoulders and lifted me to my feet. "Don't be absurd," he said. "You can't even see what you're doing. Now go on and I'll—"

"What a beautiful little pony! And he's hurt! What a shame, poor little fellow. Let me help."

Startled by the sweet, light voice, both Huard

and I turned, to find a young woman coming around the bend in the canyon wall. As melodious as the voice had been—the words were more sung than spoken—the girl was more beautiful and harmonious still. As tall as I but far more slender, hip and breast only just swelling into a woman's proportions, she had long, long hair as black as midnight and wide gray eyes. Her limbs were sleek, her hands and feet were delicately tapered and every movement was filled with unstudied grace. She came quickly forward, moving with that controlled surety that is more soothing to animals than any amount of honeyed words. Whitenose flinched as she touched him, breathed in her flower-sweet scent, and sighed, eyelids drooping lazily.

"I have quietened the pain for now," the girl told us softly, looking up into Huard's face with a kind of innocent wonder. "Will you take the other two around the turn of the canyon and into my valley? There's water and grass there and they're very thirsty."

I used my sleeve to wipe away my tears and glanced at Huard, wondering why he didn't answer. He was staring at the girl as if bespelled, dawning glory in his face. If in that moment he fell in love, I learned to hate. It was like being blasted with lightning, a bitter, poisonous bolt of withering jealousy. He had never looked at me like that. No man had ever looked at me so, and I knew with utter certainty that no man ever would.

I knew that my blighting hatred of this child-woman was unjust and cruel and unfair. The knowledge made me writhe internally with self-loathing even as jealous spite surged like bile into the back of my throat.

"I'll unload and picket them and come back to help," Huard said, and he couldn't keep the joy out of his voice even in so prosaic an utterance.

"Thank you. Please bring some stout sticks, about—oh, this long," she said, holding out her hands to show the measure. "And just turn the animals loose. My garden is fenced to keep out the dragondeer and they're welcome to whatever else they may find." She looked up at him and then away, suddenly shy. "My name is Mennefer," she added, softly.

"I'm Huard," he said. "I'll bring the sticks." For both of them, I had ceased to exist. I felt it myself, as if I were thinning into a mist and blowing away on the breeze. Even Whitenose needed me no more, now that this extraordinary young woman had taken charge. She would help him. I could only have destroyed him. I nearly choked on tears, not of sorrow for the mortal injury of a friend, but of rage and humiliation and self-pity.

Mennefer came forward and knelt by Whitenose's injured foreleg, her long black hair falling around her like a curtain. I could almost see the currents of power surging and seething as she gathered them from what source I knew not. I found it unbearable that she—she!—could save him and I could not. Mennefer began to stroke the injured place very lightly, just with the tips of her fingers, while those almost visible energies played and flowed about her and from her into Whitenose's leg.

It was only a few seconds—a minute, at most. Nor did Whitenose walk away sound. Mennefer looked up, the power fading as rapidly as it had come. "I can't mend the bone," she said, with a smile. "It will have to heal on its own. It will be some weeks before he can leave here. But I have melded the two ends firmly together, and the healing has begun."

"Thank you," I said, forcing the bitter envy back into its foul hiding place and coming forward to rub the spot behind the pony's ear that he loved to have scratched. "Thank you. He's my best friend in the world."

Mennefer gave me a startled glance. "Do you call a pony your best friend? What of your husband?"

"I have no husband . . . oh, you mean Huard. He's not my husband. He's my armsman, no more to me than that. I've known him for less than a month. I've known Whitenose for fifteen years." Why did I lie? I don't know, unless it was the same despairing bravado that sends the defeated soldier charging onto the spears of his enemy. If no one knew that I cared whether I lost Huard or not, perhaps the loss wouldn't hurt.

Whatever the reason for the lie, Mennefer accepted it as simple truth. A sweet unknown joy filled her face, where every emotion showed as clearly as the pebbly bottom of a spring-fed pool. "Then—then he has no wife, no woman of his own?" she asked, so softly I had to strain to hear.

I shrugged. It was not a question I had ever asked him—or much cared about. "I couldn't say. I can't be bothered to ferret out the personal life of an armsman."

Mennefer gave me a startled and somewhat awed glance. She obviously believed that I must have a thousand such as Huard at my beck and call to speak so contemptuously of them. I scoffed at her credulity while inwardly I cringed in terrible pain. I had never been so innocent, so trusting—how could I have been, raised a bastard amid the intrigue and deceit of a king's palace?—and I felt soiled and mean by comparison.

Huard returned with the sticks, and I made a splint, well padded with torn strips from my shabbier blanket, to immobilize the joints and allow the bruised tissues to heal while the broken ends of the bone grew together. While I did this, Huard and Mennefer stood a little apart and talked on two levels. One level, the level of words, was a simple sharing of immediate histories, but the other was deeper, spoken in a language of looks and pauses and imperceptible movements, a melding and bonding of hopes and fears and dreams. I glanced at them once as I worked. They stood together, fair and dark, Huard smiling kindly down upon Mennefer as she looked up laughing, no trace of artifice or coquettishness marring her beauty. It was as if perfection itself had been their matchmaker. I bent back to my task, trembling with rage and hatred.

When I was finished, the three of us split the pack among us and coaxed and led Whitenose around that last bend into Mennefer's valley. Oh, it was a place of beauty! It was a wide, shallow canyon, rimmed with cliffs and jumbled boulders. The narrow cleft we had followed was the bed of a seasonal stream that in spring must have spread all over the floor of the canyon, making it a shallow lake and endowing it with lushness for the rest of the year. Fruit and nut trees grew in whispering groves. From a low cliff to the left, a waterfall gushed, playing a sweet liquid melody as it bounded down a series of steps into glimmering turquoise pools, each lower than the last, until the water fed into a still lake that centered the valley like a huge dark eye. The horse and Graylegs, their thirst slaked, were grazing on the belly-deep grass with complete absorption; gallant little Whitenose threw up his head and hobbled stiff-legged to the nearest pool, where he plunged his muzzle into the water and drank until I could see his sides swell. Then he too began to eat the grass.

"Come to my castle," Mennefer said, looking up at Huard with a sweet, unconsciously adoring smile. I chose to assume that I had been included in the invitation; it would have been graceless to set up a camp here, almost in Mennefer's dooryard.

Castle, indeed! I had pictured some rude hut, charmingly rustic, shaded perhaps by one of the nut trees, maybe with a few chickens scratching in the yard. No such thing. Mennefer lived in a series of caverns hollowed out of the living rock by a million generations of flowing water, but now floored with dry sand. There were halls and chambers and rooms and winding corridors enough for a hundred people. Her main room was larger than the grand ballroom in my father's palace, and more fantastically decorated with tapestries of stained and channeled sandstone.

And the place was furnished in keeping with the magnificence of the rooms. The woods were carved and polished and darkened with age. Mennefer slept in a stone chamber in a post-

ered bed big enough for a man and his seven
wives. The bed must have been built in the
room; it was too huge to have been carried into
it. The coverlets were woven of a soft, silky
wool, which, in a finer weave, Mennefer also
wore.

There was something pathetically brave in all
this magnificence. For here Mennefer, a girl on
the verge of womanhood, bursting with life and
vitality and the sweet juice of youth, lived all
alone. She wove the fabrics to make the blankets. She toiled in her garden to grow the food,
she cooked it, and then, sitting alone at the
gleaming polished banquet table, she ate it.
With what phantasms must she have con-
versed, with what charming courtiers must her
busy mind have peopled this silent hall!

Oh, I hated her! I burned with a bitter jealousy of her beauty and her youth and her in-
nocence! I seethed with rage at the unconscious
ease with which she had captured Huard's
fickle heart! I was offended to the core of my
being that they ignored me in their absorption
with each other! And I pitied her profoundly,
and was glad for her that she had found Huard
to love—she must long ago have given up hope
that anyone would ever come wandering into
her isolated valley to whom she could give her
generous heart. If emotions had the palpable
force of magic, I would have exploded into a
million scorched and glassy fragments from the
conflict that raged within me.

She and Huard prepared supper. I went to
check on Whitenose; he had eaten to repletion
and was lying down, his splinted leg thrust
awkwardly out before him. The horse was lying

down too, and Graylegs, who had apparently been appointed sentry, dozed hipshot nearby.

At least, I told myself wryly, I could be grateful that they had remembered my existence to the point of preparing enough food for me. They talked through the meal in breathy, laughing tones, oblivious to my existence, and I ate in as much solitary state as I had sometimes seen my father do.

It was a meal without meat. There were many delicious vegetable dishes, milk to drink, and a dish of eggs. "I don't like to kill things just to eat them," Mennefer explained to Huard. "And as long as I don't have the smell of a meat-eater, I can move among the wild plant-eaters and they don't fear me." Huard, the professional hunter, gravely agreed with the wisdom of this.

Supper finished, I left them lingering over the honey-sweetened nutmeal cakes, took up a lamp, and went to search out quarters for myself. Our things were in the guest bedchamber next to Mennefer's; Huard, I supposed, had put them there while so enchanted he hardly knew what he did.

He certainly hadn't thought things through. Did he intend to court Mennefer while I shared his bed? Even she wasn't so innocent as that— at least she had her wits about her! Or did he intend to leave me in the guest bedroom and go to Mennefer this very night? Inconceivable—she would be shy and frightened, unaccustomed even to the touch of a hand. It would take long and patient courting and a slow growth of intimacy before she was ready to receive him. (As opposed to his latest lover, who had all but bullied him into servicing her, I thought, shuddering with humiliation and self-condemnation.)

But Huard was a man who could be patient and kind and gentle, and he would know better than to rush her. If I climbed into the inviting bed and went to sleep, he would just go elsewhere. And there I would be, right next to them when at last Mennefer's maidenly reluctance was overcome. No, thank you!

Besides, there was something uncanny about the room, something that gave me a shuddering aversion to it. I wouldn't have wanted to sleep there, even if things had been different.

I sorted my things out from Huard's, took the set of golden jewelry that he had bought in Termontaine out of my medicine bag, and thrust it deep into the bottom of his pack.

There were many unused rooms in Mennefer's castle, but those two were the only furnished bedrooms. I wandered through the maze of interconnected chambers and halls until I found an empty chamber far from Mennefer's bedroom and on a higher level. It had a crack through which I could see stars. It would be light in the daytime, and there was a steeply sloping ramp that led to the main chamber near the lofty opening—I could go and come as I pleased without falling all over the moonstruck pair. The mere thought of interfering in their courtship afflicted me with an almost physical nausea.

I spread my bedroll and cursed as I remembered that I had torn up my other blanket to pad the pony's splint, and had improvidently neglected to filch one of Huard's, who would have the silken-soft coverlets on the bed and wouldn't need his own. As I searched through the pack for something to protect my weary bones from the floor, which was rock on this higher level, I came across an unfamiliar parcel, carefully wrapped. For a moment, I wondered what it was. Opening it, I discovered the three blouses Huard had bought for me. I had never worn them, and now I never would. I couldn't ask Huard to button them up for me, not since Mennefer had struck him like lightning. I sat with my head bowed over the lovely, silky, impractical garments with their delicate embroidery, and grieved for the loss of something I had only thought I had.

I spent an uncomfortable night on a hard stone floor and was awake with the dawn. I went out to the lake in the stillness between first light and sunrise, when the breeze lies quietly waiting for the new day to give it direction and even the birds are only giving sleepy chirps to clear their throats. I plunged into the cold water and scrubbed and scrubbed, as if to cleanse myself of hatred and bitterness and self-pity, and came out shivering and chastened. I checked Whitenose's leg, plucked berries from Mennefer's brambles for my breakfast, and explored the area between the caverns and the lake. For a time I watched the noisy ducks come exclaiming one by one out of their nocturnal hiding places in the reeds. Then I sat in the level rays of the rising sun beside the turquoise pools and watched fat trout rise for flies, wondering if Mennefer's ban on flesh foods included fish.

"There you are! I've been hunting all over for you."

I started so that I nearly slid off the boulder from which I had been peering into the crystalline pools. "Huard," I acknowledged. "Good morning. Look at the trout! Have you ever seen

any like these with the green on their backs and
the pink spots along their sides?"

He sat down on the next rock. "Where did
you disappear to last night? I thought perhaps
you had run away."

I snorted. "And leave Whitenose? Not likely.
No, I'm a fixture here until he's well enough to
travel." Whether you and Mennefer like it or
not, I added silently.

"You took your stuff out of the bedroom," he
said.

"I was meaning to ask you if I could borrow
one of your blankets; I ripped mine up to pad
the splint yesterday."

"Where did you sleep?"

"In a high chamber to the right and up from
the main hall. I'm going to cut some grass presently to make a bed." I rubbed ruefully at a
spot on the small of my back that was still sore.

"But, Eldrie, why?"

I stubbornly refused to understand his question. "Because that rock is hard!"

"I'm not asking why you want to cut some
grass, I'm asking why you didn't sleep in the
bedroom." Huard would not be diverted.

I glanced at him. He still hadn't realized what
had happened to him. There was a glow about
him this morning, as if little sparkles were
swirling about him. "It seems like a good idea,"
I said. "Can I borrow that blanket?"

"Are you mad at me?"

"No. Look, if you don't want to lend me the
blanket I'll use one of the pack covers."

He made an impatient gesture of swatting an
annoyance aside. "Of course you can borrow a
blanket—both of them, if you like. But it isn't
right, me sleeping in the bed and you on the

floor. As you've pointed out often enough, I'm the armsman and you're the liege lady. Show me where your stuff is and I'll move it to the bedroom. I'll sleep by the gate if you think it's necessary for someone to sleep there."

"Try not to be any denser than absolutely necessary," I snapped, fed up with all this coyness. He really wanted to know if I intended to demand sexual favors from him, without asking directly lest I should interpret the question as meaning that he wanted me. And no doubt wondering how to refuse tactfully if I did. Well, let him suffer. He wouldn't suffer one tenth what I already had.

I slid down from the boulder, fetched my sword, and began using it to cut a pile of reeds. My father's arms master would have given me a hiding for using a weapon blade in such a way, but I didn't care. It felt blackly good to be killing something, even if only reeds; Huard had destroyed the precarious inner peace I had won with such a struggle.

By the time the reeds were cut and spread to dry on a flat boulder, and an even larger pile of grass had been likewise treated, I was hot and itchy. I had worked off the irritation, but a pervading melancholy had replaced it. There was only one cure—hard work, work until I dropped from exhaustion. I checked Whitenose again, slipped my medicine bag over my shoulder, and set out to explore the upper end of the valley.

Chapter Eight

✛ ✛ ✛

MENNEFER'S VALLEY was a treasure trove of medicinal plants. I spent hours in the farther reaches of the canyon, searching among the clutter of fallen boulders and slabs and crumbled cliffs. I found cliffrose, an excellent wound wash; datura, dangerous, but sometimes used to prevent miscarriage and in mental illness; fleabane, its purpose obvious from its name; globemallow, good for sore eyes; skeleton weed, for increasing the flow of milk in nursing mothers; barberry, for rheumatism; bladderpod, for snake bite; crownbeard, for skin diseases; jointfir, used (not very effectively) for syphilis; and a dozen other plants medically rare and valuable. Some of them I could identify only from having seen dried specimens in high-priced apothecary shops. I picked nothing; they were too valuable for me to take without permission. But I vowed to ask Mennefer's permission to take some if I had to throw a bucket of cold water on her to get her attention.

Such heroic measures were not necessary. I arrived back at the caverns in the twilight coolness, drank thirstily from a high rock pool no bigger than a soup tureen, and went to check Whitenose's leg. He was a little lackadaisical, a little feverish, but no more than might be expected from so severe an injury. I was walking back toward Mennefer's castle when she and Huard came toward me, almost running.

"Where have you been all day?" Huard demanded.

I gave him a dangerous look. "Walking," I said, coolly. "Did you need me for something?"

"I needed to know where you were! Don't go off like that again without telling me. Or better yet, taking me with you."

"Who do you think you are?" I asked with silky deadliness. This was more than enough. He had deserted me for a beautiful, innocent, adoring girl on two minutes' acquaintance. He had forced me to sleep on a hard rock floor with only one blanket (I was in no mood to be fair). He had tried desperately to wriggle out of having to make love to me without having the simple courage to come out and say that he no longer wanted me. He had had the audacity to question my movements—twice. And as if all that weren't enough, he was giving me—me!— orders. My hand actually went to the hilt of my sword as I stepped softly toward him, knees bent, chin thrust belligerently forward. "Just who do you think you are? Who gave you the right to know where I go and to be informed of my decisions? Do you dare overstep yourself so far, you ignorant backwoods commoner?"

I was weary—tired to death. I was smarting in all the tenderest parts of my pride—as a healer and as a woman. I was angry and lonely and I had spent the last twenty-four hours struggling heroically to subdue all the mean, petty, spiteful faults in my character. I wanted—and since it was all I could have, I felt entitled to it—deference. Respect. Apologies. A little groveling wouldn't have come amiss!

He was unarmed, and I could have run him right through and left him bleeding in the dust, and at that moment I was almost ready to do it. I wouldn't have, of course. But Mennefer darted bravely between us and stood facing me, chin up, arms extended protectively, eyes flashing.

"Please, Your Highness. Don't be angry with him. He was very worried about you. Please forgive him. He didn't mean to be disrespectful—he was overwrought."

I straightened up and snorted derisively. *He* was overwrought, was he? But my hand fell away from the hilt of my sword. Encouraged, Mennefer came hesitantly toward me. "Please, Your Highness. Surely you can forgive him for offenses committed because he loves you. Even if he is only a commoner, the love of such a man is not to be despised." She didn't understand yet what had happened to them, either, I surmised. Was I the only person here capable of seeing things as they were?

"Very well, Mennefer, since you ask it, I forgive him," I said as graciously as I could, taking a deep breath to cool the angry heat in my brain. "Huard, you've been talking out of turn again."

"Oh," he said, disconcerted. "Well, I thought—"

"I know what you thought," I interrupted. How could he keep secrets from this girl, of all girls in the world? "Never mind. Did you save me something to eat?"

"We haven't eaten yet," Mennefer said eagerly. "We were waiting for you. I'll go and fix it now." She dashed away, running with lithe grace.

"Don't hurry, I need a bath," I called after her.

"Eldrie, I don't understand what's happened to you," Huard complained. "You won't tell me what's wrong and you're as touchy as a bear with a toothache."

I sighed, defeated by his denseness. "Huard, I only want Whitenose to be well. Then I want to get out of here. There isn't anything you can do about what's the matter with me."

"Don't you want to learn to be a healing mage any more?"

"No. Now go away, I want to take a bath and then I have to get those reeds and grass up to my room before it gets too dark to see."

"We fixed you a bed. If you don't mind, I'll bathe with you." We had bathed together several times when we had been lovers. It had been a lot of fun and inevitably led to other things. Huard was testing me, I knew, to see if I was determined to pursue him.

"No!" I said sharply. "I want to bathe alone. Go away."

"Eldrie, I don't understand!" he said violently. "Why, all of a sudden, are you acting like I've contracted some incurable disease? I'm still your loyal liegeman!"

"All right, you're still in my liegeman, though you know you can have your oath back for the asking. But you aren't my lover anymore, Huard. I don't want to—I can't—discuss it. This is all hard enough without keeping on and on about it."

"Can't you even tell me why? Have I offended you? Was I too rough with you? You haven't found someone you want more—there isn't anyone here!"

I turned and walked away from him toward the lake. He would never see the tears in my eyes. "No, Huard," I called over my shoulder. "It's nothing you've done, and there isn't anyone else." No, there wasn't anyone, not in this valley, not in the whole world.

"I won't take my oath back!" he shouted fiercely.

Supper was a silent meal. As we finished our dessert, I turned to Mennefer. "You're a wonderful cook," I said warmly. It was not the child's fault that I disliked her so much. I would have to be extra gracious to her to make up for it.

"Thank you," she said shyly. "I'm sure you've had many more elaborate meals in your father's palace."

"Oh, yes, more elaborate, though the children ate in the nursery and I was hardly more than a child when I left. But I've never had a better meal. Mennefer, there are some very valuable plants in the canyons and on the cliffs at the far end of your valley. I was wondering if you'd mind if I took some."

"Pick whatever you like," she said. "The plants don't belong to me. How do you mean, valuable? Are they worth a lot of money?"

"They're valuable as medicines," I explained. "Some of them might be worth a bit of money, I suppose, in an apothecary's shop. But I want them for their medicinal uses. Some of them are rare elsewhere, and hard to find. I'm an herb doctor."

"Oh!" she said. "An herb doctor! Will you teach me something about the herbs you find? Healing magic is so limited—I've often longed to know about medicines and treatments."

"I'll be glad to teach you. And now, if you'll excuse me, I'll go to bed. I've had a long day. Good night." I avoided Huard's eyes as I took a lamp and headed for my chamber.

Huard had been telling the truth when he told me they had fixed me a bed. They had made a simple frame by notching and lashing small logs together. Then they had woven smaller, springy branches across these. My reeds, nicely dried, were laid across this yielding base, and a mattress of down over that. Several of the soft, silky woolen blankets had been used to make up the bed, and pillows stuffed with sweet-scented, rustly dry grass were piled at the head. I sank into this delicious comfort with a sigh of weary pleasure.

But I found it hard to sleep. My mind mulled tenaciously over the events of the day. There was something amiss, though I couldn't quite pin it down to its source. It had something to do with Huard's actions. He was clearly falling in love with Mennefer, and as clearly, his admiration was returned. Then why was he not content to accept gratefully the freedom from my bed I had offered? He felt no desire for me any longer; maybe he never had. To resume our relationship here would certainly injure his chances with Mennefer, who hadn't outgrown the absurd sensitivity of adolescence.

I knew Huard well enough now that he could no more hide his feelings from me than one of the ponies could, and I knew that these things were true. Furthermore, Huard was no fool, and certainly not so far out of touch with his own feelings as to mistake his growing affection and passion for Mennefer for the comfort and companionship he and I shared—he wouldn't be likely to mistake a cozy candle for the blazing sun! Then why had he protested when I broke off the relationship that was now only an inconvenience to him?

It didn't make sense.

I took Mennefer the *Encyclopaedia Medica* in the morning. "There are several very good articles about the principles of herbal medicine in this," I told her. "And many of the plants I found yesterday are discussed in great detail in articles of their own."

She reached out and touched the book, running her finger hesitantly over the calfskin cover. "Oh," she said. "But I can't read. I never had the need to learn and there are no books here. Can't you show me the plants and tell me what they're for? I have a good memory."

"Have you lived here all your life, then?" I asked, realizing that her experience was limited indeed if that were so.

"Nearly. I've been to the town three times. And I wasn't born here. I was a sickly baby and my mother brought me here when everyone had given up hope that I would live. The healing mage who lived here then cured me, but my mother died. As she had never told the mage who my father was or where she was from, the mage kept me here and raised me upon the milk of dragondeer. She taught me all I needed to know."

"Then the arts of the healing mages can be taught? They don't have to be inborn?"

"The power must be present to some degree. The skill to focus and direct it can be learned."

"Could I learn it?"

Without answering, Mennefer placed her cool fingers on my forehead. I felt a tingling that brought a shiver down my backbone. "No," Mennefer said with certitude. "You have a very great power, but it is not the healing power. I don't know what it is. I've never felt anything like it."

"It's the power of the royal gifts," Huard said. Neither of us had heard him come in. "It can strengthen or overmaster any other kind of power."

"Nonsense," I said sharply. "I'm going wildcrafting today. I'll return this evening and show you how to use the plants I've found."

"I'll go with you," Huard said promptly, regret in the glance he cast at Mennefer. He thought I couldn't see it.

"No, thank you," I said. "I'll take Graylegs to carry the plants back. And I have my sword. You stay here and make yourself useful."

"You might need—"

"I said, I will go alone," I said softly. Even I heard the unaccustomed ring of authority in my voice. I could not command my own lover, I realized. I liked a man to take the dominant role in bed and Huard, especially, was too vigorously masculine to be able to take orders from his woman. But I was no longer his woman. And if he was not my lover, then he was nothing to me but my liegeman. I could command my armsman, and he must obey.

Huard felt the change in me. Involuntarily, he assumed a respectfully straight posture, halted in his protest as if by a bolt of lightning. Even Mennefer, at whom the words had not been directed, felt their authority. She shrank back against the table, eyes wide. I glanced once at each of them, catching their eyes. I would be obeyed.

I worked hard that day, picking and sorting and digging and packing. In the heat and discomfort, in the weariness of labor, I sought to grind out the poison of jealousy and hatred. By day's end, I had at least made a start. It was as if the corrosive acid generated by those loathsome emotions were working out to the surface, I mused wryly, inspecting my blistered hands. And I had garnered an impressive collection of botanicals that could be made up into a variety of useful medicines. Out of evil might yet come good, if I could just master my baser self.

I came into the cavern quietly, unseen in the full dark already covering the valley, and unheard. I saw before me a tender scene. Huard and Mennefer were sitting in the pool of light cast by a single oil lamp. As delicately as a flower turning toward the sun, Huard was leaning over to kiss Mennefer, his lips just touching hers, floating above them, drawing away. Her eyes were enormous, startled, wondering.

"There, that wasn't so bad, was it?" I heard him say, his voice gentle.

"Oh, no," she said. "Is that all there is to it?"

I withdrew in haste, pursued by Huard's happy chuckle. In this very private moment, I was an intruder. I was hungry, but the only way into the kitchen was past the courting couple and I had gone to bed dinnerless before this. I groped my way up the passage to my room in the dark. The effort of finding flint and steel in the profound darkness and of striking a light was beyond me; I undressed by feel and crept into my bed.

How I envied them their happiness, at the same time I realized more poignantly than ever before that kind of happiness was not for me. I might take a lover, might glory in him for a few weeks, a few months, even perhaps a year. But in time I would become bored. Some laughing, ramshackle adventurer would pass my way, a twinkle in his eye; or some grave, dignified, sober-sided burgher would amaze himself by his unaccustomed passion when I gave him a side-long smiling look; or some blushing, sweet lad would stammer out his shy adoration; and my interest would stray. No, there was none of life-long loves, home, hearth, and children for me.

I could not but be glad for Mennefer, even as I writhed on my pillow with jealousy. Huard was the first lover that every girl dreams about and very few ever get. He would be gentle with her. He would explain to her what he was do-ing. He would be patient with her fears and her ignorance, and he would convince her that she was the very most desirable and loving woman in all the world—and every shy virgin wants to be thought impossibly skilled by her lover.

What a contrast with my own first experi-ence! My craft mistress and I had been staying in a town in the Forelt; there was plenty of work there. I had been nearly ready to leave her and strike out on my own as a healer, and she had not scrupled to send me out on the simpler cases. There was a woman, wife of a cloth wholesaler, who had too little to do and a dis-position to be ailing (not the same thing as an ailing disposition). I went to her every day with some new potion for her vast array of imagi-nary ills. The merchant's house was behind his shop, and he spoke to me pleasantly as I passed through every day. He was a friendly man, old enough to be my father, or considering how very young my own father had been when I was born, my grandfather—about fifty, I suppose, which seemed a vast age to me at eighteen.

If he wasn't busy, he would invite me into his private office, and we would laugh together and drink a cup of tea. I liked him; he had a wry sense of humor and a quick mind, and when he kissed me one day, I made no objection. "Eldrie," he said, smiling with gentle self-deprecation, "I should like to make love to you. I know I seem very old to you, but you're as fresh and lively and exciting a girl as I've ever known. I want you, Eldrie, and I need you. Will you come to me tonight?"

I was curious. I had done a little adolescent exploration with my friend in the stables, Janni, but he had flatly refused to go any farther than some hasty and nervous kissing and touching—and I had had practically to bully him to do that. And I liked the merchant. I knew that his wife had denied him her bed several years ago, for she had told me about it—she called the act of love "all that." I looked into his face, and saw for the first time the signs of aroused desire there: the shortened breath, the slight flush, the intentness of the eyes, and knew that he did want me. The knowledge awoke an answering desire in me and I nodded. "I'll come," I whispered.

He kissed me quickly. "Good girl! Come after dark to the shop door and tap. I often work late at my books and no one will think anything about it."

When I tapped on the door, it was opened quickly and I was almost snatched through the narrow gap. I was hastened into a storage room, and there, on a pile of bolts of cloth, my curiosity concerning what men and women did together was satisfied, though I was left wondering why anyone bothered. I was bustled

out and thrust through the partly open door
again; I don't think more than ten minutes had
passed since I entered. Nor did the man guess
that I was a virgin, I'm sure. There was little
blood and the whole thing was over too quickly
for me to feel any pain.

The next day as I passed through the shop,
the merchant was curt, almost brusque, in his
greeting, and kept his face averted. I saw the
mingled shame and disgust in his expression,
though, and my heart recoiled. When I saw his
wife, I knew at once that he had gone to her
and confessed his guilt, and I was let to know
that I was no longer wanted in that house.
Clearly she regarded me as the aggressor. I suppose the merchant had told her so to excuse his
infidelity.

Mennefer would be spared any such degrad-
ing experience. I was glad for that, even while
I almost chewed the pillows in an agony of lust
and loneliness, for which in this valley there
was no relief. I wasn't tired enough, I decided
grimly. Tomorrow I would have to work harder
and longer, so that I dropped into my bed completely exhausted.

No one was astir in the morning when I went
cautiously down to the main room. I slipped
out, examined Whitenose, and rewrapped his
leg after a good rubbing to promote the circu-
lation. "Get well fast, little fellow," I told him.
"I must, must get out of here soon or I shall go
mad. And I absolutely will not leave you for her
to have too!"

I left the plants I had gathered the day before
draped over Mennefer's garden fence to dry.
Taking Graylegs again, with empty packs, I hurried to the far end of the valley. This time I

clambered up the crumbling cliffs to the high plateau that backed them. I walked at least ten miles at such a driving pace that poor little Graylegs had to trot to keep up. Then I set to work, collecting quantities of sage, brittlebush, creosote, and other plants that grew on this high, windswept, dry plateau.

I nearly fainted from weakness before I realized that I hadn't eaten since yesterday morning. There were numbers of rabbits here, and although I would have respected Mennefer's dietary preferences down in the valley, up here was unclaimed land and I could do as I liked. A snare that Huard had taught me how to set caught me a meal. While it was roasting, I made myself a strong, bitter cup of sage tea, which was said to suppress excessive sexual desire; I'd never noticed any such effect in myself, but I had never had such need of it, either. It was worth a try. There were a few mariposas about, and I gathered the small bulbs, though it was risky—they were almost indistinguishable from death-lilies. In my present reckless and melancholy mood, I didn't much care if they were death-lilies. They weren't, though, and I baked them in the coals and ate them with the lean dry roasted rabbit.

The meal finished and half the rabbit wrapped up and stowed in my pack for supper, I went back to work, keeping myself furiously at it until the westering sun warned me that I must get back to the crumbling cliffs if I were to have daylight with which to pick my way down. I ate as I walked, casting the bones aside, and managed to get down into the valley in the last afterglow of sunset. I went directly to Whitenose, rubbed his leg again, all but fell into the lake to bathe, and crept back into the cavern in full darkness, my legs twitching with weariness. My last thought as I sank into my bed was that I would have to spend tomorrow preparing medicines from the plants I had gathered for the last two days or they would spoil and be wasted. I would have to ask Mennefer for oil and honey and beeswax, for which I could pay her with a liberal supply of prepared medicines.

I slept a little later the next morning, and arose stiff and cranky. After massaging Whitenose's leg again, I gathered my plants, loaded Graylegs with as much as he could carry, and made my way to the other side of the lake. Here I set to work, making packets of teas. I made mixtures of dried herbs which could be boiled to make infusions. I pounded and rubbed roots and leaves on a flat slab of sandstone to make powders for dusting wounds. I was careful, as I worked, to chant the appropriate healing spells into each medicine; they weren't half as effective without the magic. It was nearly noon before I saw any sign of life around the cavern.

For all either of them knew, I thought crossly, I could have been dead and rotting for these three days. I sought Mennefer out in the kitchen, where she was baking honey cakes. There was a misty glow about her and a contented little smile playing about her lips—no mistaking what had happened to her. "Mennefer," I said, loudly.

She had been looking in my direction, but she jumped and dropped her wooden spoon anyway. "Oh!" she said, her gaze focusing on me. "Princess Eldrie! Why, there you are! We've been very worried about you."

I'll just bet you have, I said to myself wryly.
Aloud I said, "I'd like to trade you some prepared medicines for some oil, some honey, and
a good supply of beeswax. And whatever Huard
has been telling you, I'm not a princess. If you
have to give me a title, mine is Eldrie Fitzroi.
But I prefer not to use it—it isn't exactly an
honor, you know."

"Oh, but—but, well—you can have whatever
you need. Come and I'll show you the storeroom and you can just help yourself whenever
you like."

"I don't want to short you for the winter."

"Oh, you won't, I'm not—I mean, this year's
harvest isn't in yet. You can have all you want."

So Huard has promised to take her away with
him, I thought. Well, good luck to them. I followed her to the dark chamber, where there
were earthen jars of honey still in the comb,
firkins of nut oil, dried fruit, grain ready to be
ground into flour, and many other supplies—
enough for a dozen people. I took several jars
of honey, a piece of linen for straining the beeswax, and a large firkin of oil. "Thank you," I
said. "I'll leave you a good supply of medicines
and I'll draw pictures of the parts of the body
they're used for on the outside of the jars."

She came out of her dream with a little start.
"That would be fine," she said, and drifted away.

I went up to my room, fetched a small jar
from my pack, and went to find Huard. He was
sitting by one of the rock pools, staring dreamily into the water, smiling.

"Huard," I said. Sure enough, he jumped.
Then he looked at me, blushed, looked away,
stood up, and sat down.

"Eldrie," he said weakly.

"Huard, this is a jar of my contraceptive cream. If Mennefer uses it before you have intercourse with her, it will prevent pregnancy." I held out the jar.

I had expected a little blushing and stammering—after all, he had dumped me for the girl. What I got was a cold offended stare. "Mennefer would be proud to bear my child," he said, stressing the name.

Baffled, I let my hand fall. "But surely you don't want to leave her with a baby to raise," I said helplessly.

"I wouldn't leave her. She knows that. And *she* doesn't think I'm too common to father her child."

"For heaven's sake, do you think I thought that?"

"Well, you certainly took care to avoid the possibility. It didn't bother you any to make me wait while you fixed yourself up."

I lost my temper. "Don't be an idiot. How do you think I'd raise a baby, traveling around the way I do?" I snapped. "It never occurred to me that you wanted to father a child on me. Pretty inconsiderate, I call it."

"What man wouldn't like to think that his son might be a king?" he growled. "What man wants to think that a woman thinks he's good enough to lie with but doesn't want his baby?"

"Huard," I said with exaggerated patience, "it wasn't your baby I didn't want, it was any baby. And if you had gotten me pregnant, the poor little tyke would have had about as much chance of becoming a king as your horse over there. The bastard son of a bastard, become a king? Come on."

"He wouldn't have been a bastard."

"Oh, yes, he would have. You may be good in bed, but I certainly wouldn't have married you," I said, knowing that it was a cruel and ugly thing to say. "And even if I had, he still wouldn't have been in line for the throne. I have two legitimate half-brothers who probably have sons of their own by now, and should they all be wiped out in some unimaginable disaster, my father is perfectly capable of siring more sons."

Huard rose slowly from his rock. "Eldrie, you're angry with me on account of Mennefer," he said. "I don't blame you. You had every right to assume that I belonged to you. How can I explain to you what happened?"

"No need," I said wearily. "I saw it happening. I won't claim my feelings weren't hurt, because they were. But after all, it was I who seduced you. I suppose I shouldn't have been surprised that you fell in love with Mennefer; I knew perfectly well that you didn't love me. And I owe you an apology for saying that about marrying you. It was cruel and unnecessary."

He looked down at the ground. "No," he said quietly. "You didn't seduce me. I tricked you into coming to me, that's all. It's one of the hunter's gifts, to know how to get the quarry to walk willingly into the trap." I stared at him in surprise. "You didn't think that royalty were the only ones to have gifts, did you? In Nordron, we say that everyone has gifts according to their true calling. I have the hunter's gift. Mennefer has the healer's gift. And you have the king's gifts."

I dismissed this as so much superstitious nonsense, though I was going to have to think about the matter of whether I had seduced him or he had tricked me into his bed. "Well," I said stiffly, "you'll have to do as you think best about the contraceptive, of course. Here it is, in case you want it." I put the jar down on a rock. "As soon as Whitenose is healed enough to travel, I'll be on my way, and in the meantime, I have plenty to do gathering plants and brewing medicines. You won't see me often." I turned away.

I worked hard for the next few days. Often I packed Graylegs with a light camping outfit and spent the night beside some stagnant pool of alkaline water, having walked twenty miles or more during the day. I ate what I could catch or find. Both Graylegs and I grew hard and gaunt, and I tanned and wind-burned until I was as brown as the shells of the hazelnuts that grew in Mennefer's valley. I gathered hundreds of pounds of botanicals. I talked to the pony often, but the sound of any other human voice grew to be strange and startling to me.

Occasionally, out of necessity, I spent the day manufacturing medicines and reading the *Encyclopaedia Medica* at my "workshop" on the far side of the lake from the cavern. It was upon one of these days that Huard and Mennefer came strolling around the lake, hand in hand. I watched them come, sighing enviously as I saw how comfortable they had become with each other, like an old married couple. Reminding myself sharply that I was by nature unsuited to that particular kind of felicity, I rose to meet them.

"Hello, Eldrie," Huard said, looking me up and down. "What have you been doing to yourself? You're thin as a rail. Be sure and come for supper tonight."

"Thank you, no," I said. I could accept that Huard and Mennefer had found a kind of con-

tentment together that I could hardly understand, much less aspire to, but I found it
inexplicably painful to watch them together, so
tenderly solicitous of each other as they were.
The few meals I had attended at the cavern had
exacerbated my loneliness unendurably. "I have
a decoction brewing that I have to watch. Good
evening, Mennefer."

She dropped a graceful curtsy. "Good evening, Your Highness. Did I do that right?"

"Yes, it was well done, but not to the right
person. I have no right to the title nor to the
courtesy."

"Eldrie, Mennefer is taking me to see the
dragons tomorrow," Huard said. "Please come
with us."

"Yes, do, please," Mennefer seconded, smiling winningly at me. "I think there may be a
young one. They don't calve very often; this is
a rare opportunity."

"You've been working too hard," Huard said,
looking at the ranks of jars and the tottering
piles of packets of teas and powders. "You already have more than the two ponies can carry.
You need a day of relaxation. Come with us."

"Dragons?" I said, looking from one to the
other, suspicious for a moment that they were
playing some joke on me. "Real living dragons?
I thought they were only a myth."

"No, though I think they may soon become
extinct," Mennefer said. "They're a beautiful
sight. Not many people can say they've seen the
dragons. Won't you come with us?"

"Besides, poor old Graylegs needs a rest too.
You could hang your hat on his hipbones,"
Huard added.

This was undeniably true, and I did want to

see the dragons—very much! Perhaps a day spent in the company of the two lovers need not be too impossibly uncomfortable if I just avoided looking at them. "Well," I said.

"Oh, wonderful! You will come! I'll go and make a special dinner to celebrate. Huard, would you like to stay and help Eldrie put away her medicines? Then you could walk over to supper with her later."

She darted away without waiting for an answer, and Huard began gathering bunches of dried herbs. There was no decoction simmering on the fire, but he tactfully forebore to mention it. "We haven't seen much of you lately," he said, busy with his work. "You seldom sleep in your room and you almost never come in for meals. Have you been lonely?"

"Certainly not. I've been busy. The ponies are all the company I need."

"Good. I thought perhaps you were staying away because our company was unpleasant to you. I'm glad to know it was only because you had so much to do."

I glanced at him, suspicious of sarcasm, but his expression was bland. "There," he said. "I think that's everything. You know, this would be easier to do in Mennefer's kitchen. Then you wouldn't have so far to carry things to put them in out of the weather." I had taken over the chamber nearest my bedroom for a storeroom.

"Some of the medicines give off quite a stench when brewing," I said. "It seemed more considerate not to smell up Mennefer's home."

He nodded. "That was thoughtful." There was a stilted and awkward feel about the whole conversation, and I could no longer sense his feelings. We had become strangers to each other once again.

Mennefer had outdone herself in the preparation of the meal, considering the limited number of ingredients she had to draw upon. They were both determined to include me in their conversation (I imagined them discussing me—"Poor old Eldrie, she feels left out. Let's be sure to talk to her at supper tonight." "Good idea, she must be awfully lonely. We'll ask her to go to see the dragons with us tomorrow"). I'd have been more comfortable if they'd just left me alone. I excused myself to go to bed right after the meal.

Chapter Nine
✣ ✣ ✣

THE DRAGONS WERE incredibly beautiful. From the fairy tales of my childhood, I had expected scaly reptilian monsters. These dragons were clearly mammals, more closely related to bats than to snakes. Take a flying fox. Magnify him a thousand times. Stretch him out to an attenuated thinness almost beyond imagining, giving him a long arching neck and tapered tail. Clothe him with rich auburn fur, patterned with chestnut dapples. Give him foot-long fangs so sharp and gleaming they positively sing with keenness. Put great curving claws on the wrist joint of his wings, with which he can cling to a cliff face like some huge incredible living tapestry, or walk four-legged upon the ground. Then you would have an approximation of a dragon—but you still wouldn't have the grace, the awe, the beauty of the living creatures before us. We crouched on the rim of a canyon and watched them, fascinated.

"I thought dragons had four legs and wings," Huard whispered.

"I thought so too," I whispered back. "But now that I see these, it makes sense. They're animals like us. If they had six limbs, I suppose they'd be a kind of insect."

"Look at their eyes," Mennefer said softly. "They have wise eyes. They aren't insects, or snakes either."

She was right. The eyes of these enormous creatures were almost human, set in the front of their faces above their toothy muzzles. I had seen monkeys and apes often in circuses and menageries; these dragons had much the same look about them, as if an alien sapience dwelt in their narrow skulls. They weren't relatives of the bats, either. They were primates, and thus our own cousins.

One leaped away from the cliff wall, stretching out its wings with a crack like thunder, tilting as it scooped the wind into the vast membranes. They were so delicate! It was easy to see, now that one was in flight, why they had been mistaken for serpents; this one must have had a wingspan of sixty feet, yet it could have weighed no more than a hundred and fifty pounds. It was all membrane and fur and gleaming fangs.

I realized, with a lurch of my heart, that it had seen us. It banked and swooped, inspecting us as it went by. Seeming to find in us neither prey nor danger, it sailed away, climbing above the canyon by some magic, or perhaps a rising wind.

"Look!" Mennefer whispered excitedly. "There's the baby!"

Sure enough, a small one was being carefully shepherded toward the little stream that wound through the middle of the wide canyon floor. It was still wobbly on its legs and its wing membranes were crumpled. It would be a long time before the little creature would be able to fly. Its mother, too, gave the impression of being earthbound. Her breasts, placed on her chest like a human woman's, were swollen with milk. She looked as if caring for a newborn dragon were exhausting work.

There were herds of the deerlike creatures, such as Mennefer kept for their milk, smaller than goats, with sharp spiky little horns. They were grazing upon the grass of the canyon floor; one of the other dragons, another female, strode toward one of the herds with a shoulder-swinging, hunching gait. She inspected the animals carefully. Then, as delicately as a lady picking a candied cherry off a plate, she plucked one of the deer out of the herd, crunched it expertly, and ate it. The rest of the herd seemed sublimely unaware that one of their mates was gone, continuing to eat the grass busily. The dragon picked up another deer, crunched it, and took it to the new mother, still crouching at the edge of the water. She accepted the tidbit gratefully.

We continued to watch, bemused and enthralled by the ethereal beauty of the creatures. Dragon was too harsh a word for them. There should have been a more musical term.

"These are all there are," Mennefer told us sadly.

I was horrified. "All? Anywhere?" I counted them. There were four females and three males, including the one that had flown. And the infant.

"As far as I know, there are no more dragons, anywhere. Certainly not in the known world. And still men continue to hunt them, for their flesh, which is said to convey wisdom, and for their pelts and the membranes of their wings. They grow fewer every year."

"If I really were royal," I declared, "I would make a law protecting them."

"The royal writ of Maritiene doesn't extend this far," Huard pointed out.

"No. Nor could I use it if it did," I retorted.

The light of battle was in Huard's eye; I was only spared an argument by Mennefer's sudden, "Hush! Look! Something's happening!"

The big male that had flown was coming back, but he was flying erratically, flapping his wings raggedly where once he had soared. The other two males sprang into the air and beat their way up to meet him, calling agitatedly, while the females on the ground stretched up their necks to watch him. Their calls were like the sound of trumpets, underlaid with the reverberations of great bells.

The male wheeled crazily to a landing, sprawling with one wing spread out on the grassy ground like a fallen tent. Even from the cliff above, we could see the bellows-heaving of his broad chest, the trembling of his flanks, the face twisted into a grimace of pain. "Oh!" cried Mennefer. "He's hurt!" And before either of us could stop her, she slid over the lip of the cliff

and scrambled down it in a rain of dislodged
pebbles and sand.

A vivid image of the crunching of the little
deer flashed across my mind's eye. There was
nothing more dangerous to approach than a
wounded animal, and of all animals, surely
there was none more dangerous than a dragon!
"Stay there!" I ordered Huard, and I used a
tone of command. I knew, without knowing how
I knew, that he would be frozen in his place for
a few minutes. He literally could not disobey
me. And I also knew that I could, for a few precious seconds, command the dragons. Perhaps
for long enough to save his love for him.

Over the verge of the cliff I went, and for the
next few seconds, all my attention was on feet
and hands and little nubs and cracks in the
rock. Then my feet hit the level ground. I looked
around. Mennefer was running across the canyon floor toward the injured dragon, her midnight hair rippling behind her. The dragons
were raising startled heads, swiveling eyes and
ears in her direction, baring fangs and spreading wings.

I pelted after her. I was fast, and in rock-hard
condition; I was catching up with her rapidly.
Suddenly she stopped and went down to one
knee. "Let me help you," I heard her pleading.
"Please let me help you!"

The injured dragon turned his dazed eyes on
her. The fangs glittered as he drew back his lips
in a defiant snarl. The other dragons lurched as
they swung toward her, teeth bared. I leaped in
front of her. Holding up both hands, I gathered
my voice as if it were a trailing garment.
"Stop!" I commanded. I didn't say it loudly, but
the air rang with the word nevertheless, and

the canyon echoed with it as if it had been the shout of thousands. The dragons threw back their startled heads, trumpeting—brass and flutes and the tolling of huge bells. Even the wounded dragon groaned aloud and twisted his neck.

"Good!" exclaimed Mennefer. "Hold them!"

I dared not move or speak. Only the force of my will was holding back the rage of these awesome beasts, and that for only a few precarious seconds, until they overcame their amazement. And Mennefer, with sublime and completely unjustified confidence in my powers, was walking coolly up to an injured and enraged dragon. No! I longed to call to her. No! Run! Run to Huard who loves you! I cannot hold these uncanny beasts for more than a few seconds! If you don't run, you'll die, and I'll have sacrificed myself for nothing! But I could only stare into the great eyes of the dragons, so like those of men and women that as I lost all sense of perspective I thought I was staring into human eyes, eyes with wisdom and knowledge and great sadness behind them.

I don't know how long I stood frozen, locked in motionless combat of will with the winged creatures. They towered above me, swaying like hypnotized snakes. Peripherally, I was aware of Mennefer moving about the wounded dragon, which was stretched limply on the grass, eyes half closed. I knew when the energy began to spark around her as it had when she treated Whitenose, only a thousand times stronger. Then the universe dissolved into a swirling storm of gray flecks and the sapient eyes of dragons. I remembered that in the fairy tales it was said to be dangerous to look into the eyes of dragons.

"Eldrie, Eldrie. It's done. Come, we can go now. They'll let us go." It was Mennefer, plucking at my sleeve, pulling me away. The universe lurched and settled, and I glanced away from the dragons' eyes. The sun was halfway down the horizon; it had stood at the zenith when the dragons had begun to call. Mennefer was white and drained, swaying with fatigue. I put my arm around her to help her along, and was surprised to find that I was as weak as she. Together, we dragged back to the cliff, and along it, looking for a place to climb it—in our condition, there was no question of going back up the way we had come down. We came to a place where a seasonal stream had worn away a channel in the rock, and, clinging to the crumbling walls, were able to clamber painfully back up to the anxious Huard.

He picked Mennefer up in his arms. "Can you make it?" he said to me, his eyes on Mennefer's pinched face. Her head sank down on his shoulder, the closed eyelids smudged with blue veins in their transparency.

"Yes," I said, since there was no other possible answer. I couldn't stay here and Huard certainly couldn't carry both of us.

He set off in the direction of Mennefer's valley. This was unknown land to me; all my explorations had been to the east of the valley and the dragons' canyon was to the south. I gritted my teeth and set myself to the overwhelmingly difficult task of placing one foot before the other.

Even burdened as he was, Huard quickly outdistanced me. I wasn't in any pain and I had often been more tired. But I had never been so weak. I was as limp as if the blood had all been drained out of me. My knees wobbled with every step; I had to concentrate to keep them from buckling. When I tried to lift my hand to steady myself on a boulder as I passed, I couldn't muster the energy to raise it and bumped my hip painfully on the rough rock. Presently I realized that I was kneeling in the hot sand with no very clear idea of how I had gotten there.

I thought about the effort required to rise to my feet. It was a daunting task, one I contemplated without enthusiasm. I dared not sit or lie down. If I got any lower than I was already, I felt I would never rise again. I put my palms down on the sand before me; it was so hot that they were stung by the heat. I wished that I had fallen in the shade of the boulder on my left, only a few feet away, but it was much too far to crawl. A sand serpent came whispering past, its scales rustling dryly against the sand. It flicked its tongue at me and poured itself away between two rocks.

I wished we had brought Graylegs with us. He would have stood quietly while I pulled myself up his leg or his tail, and then allowed me to cling to his mane as we walked along. I ran my tongue over my dry lips. Huard had the canteen. It was entirely reasonable that he should have gone off carrying Mennefer, but I really felt that he might have left me the canteen.

Presently the sun dropped behind the rim of the gorge and the coolness was so refreshing that I was able to scramble awkwardly to my feet and begin once again to follow the dented footprints in the sand. I was surprised, after a time, to hear a galloping horse come up the canyon from the direction of Mennefer's valley. Had one of the animals strayed? It occurred to me that I was right in its way and that I had better move over to the wall of the canyon if I wished to avoid being trampled. But it was a long way—three extra steps, at least—and I hated to lengthen my journey by so much.

Huard's horse came pounding around the bend, throwing up a spray of stinging sand. Huard was on his back, too. He pulled the sweating beast to a stop.

"Where are you going in such a hurry?" I asked, looking up at him.

"I came to get you," he said.

"Why?" I asked, faintly alarmed. Something must have happened to have inspired him to such haste.

He slid off the horse's back, giving me an exasperated look. "Because you need help getting home," he said.

"No, I don't," I reassured him. "Now that it's cooler I'm fine. You might have left me the canteen, though. I'm thirsty."

He held out his interlaced hands to give me a leg up on the horse. "We'll be home in just a few minutes. Up you go."

"I don't want to ride with you, Huard."

"No," he said, slowly, "I daresay you don't, and I can't blame you for it. But you're going to anyway."

"I'm quite capable of walking."

"Maybe. But you're going to ride. Come on." With that, he seized me on either side of my waist and tossed me up. Before I could do anything about it, he had leaped up and wheeled the huge beast, kicking him into a wallowing gallop. I was too jolted and tossed around to do anything more than cling to the woolly mane; when I started to order him to put me down, I accidentally bit my tongue.

It wasn't long before he was drawing rein before the cavern entrance. I slid down before he could help me and made stiffly for the cool hanging jar of water that Mennefer kept in a breezy spot. I drank deeply, feeling my sun-dried tissues expanding. Then I headed for the sloping passage that led to my room. I should have checked to see that Mennefer was well, I supposed, but Huard could take care of her—that was where he should have been, instead of galloping through the canyons rescuing people who didn't want to be rescued.

I fell across the bed fully dressed, to be awakened some time later when someone pulled off my boots. I grumbled sleepily, was hushed and covered up. Had the voice not been masculine, I would have thought that time had reversed itself and my nurse was tucking me into my bed in the royal nursery.

I awoke in the morning tired and lethargic. It was full daylight out; I had planned to go wild-crafting, since Graylegs had had two full days of rest. But it was too late; the day's heat was far advanced, and I wouldn't be able to travel beyond the areas I had already collected. I would just have to spend the day here in Mennefer's valley. Well, I could wash and mend my clothes; they were past due for it. I gathered them up.

The two shirts were dirty—it was a toss-up whether I ought to wash them or bury them. So were both pairs of trousers. I searched around for something to wear while I did my laundry.

My glance fell on the package of blouses Huard
had bought for me. They were clean and new;
perhaps I could contort myself enough to fasten the buttons. The skirts were still in the pack.
I dug out the package they were in and took one
out, selecting the blue set. Then I slipped into
my dirty clothes and carried the fresh down to
the lake. I stripped off the old clothes and put
them to soak, weighting them down with stones,
while I bathed with slow luxury. Then I dressed
in the new clothes, nearly dislocating my shoulder blades—but I got them buttoned. It was
easier than I had anticipated; they were a lot
looser on me than they would have been a few
weeks before.

Clean and presentable at last, I left the
clothes to soak and walked up to the caverns,
moving slowly in the heeled slippers so as not
to sprain an ankle. As I came into the main hall,
Huard and Mennefer rose from the table and
came toward me. Absurdly, Huard bowed and
Mennefer curtsied; Huard hurried to the end of
the table and held the great carven chair that
was placed there. No one had sat there since
we had come to this cursed beautiful valley; I
was being offered the place as a tribute to the
rank Huard insisted upon investing with me. I
was too tired and hungry to argue. I took the
chair, nodding my thanks.

Mennefer, looking remarkably rested, re-
freshed, and lovely even after her heroic exer-
tions of the day before, scurried in from the
kitchen with dishes, which she placed before
me. Huard gravely helped me to generous por-
tions of each, standing behind my chair on the
left as I had seen my father's chamberlain do.
And as my father had done, I accepted a dish

with a nod or waved one away. Mennefer, standing by the tunnel that led to the kitchen, watched, carried plates and bowls away and brought new ones.

"An excellent meal, Mennefer," I said graciously, laying aside my napkin. If they wanted it so much, I would play their little game of royalty, though I found it sad and disheartening to have such an uncomfortable distance placed between me and my only associates. It was beyond me why so many people dreamed and schemed to attain royal honors. Didn't they know how lonely and boring it was, being treated forever as someone apart and different? The life of a traveling healer, with its excitement and variety, was infinitely preferable.

"Thank you, Your Highness," she said, as suddenly shy as if she had never seen me before. She had not, I suddenly realized, planned to attach my erstwhile lover's affections and to leave me alone and lonely. It had never occurred to her that I had the same simple human needs as any other woman. And by detaching myself from their company, I had fostered her mistake. I should have stayed and fought for Huard. I would have lost, but I wouldn't have distanced myself so profoundly. I had somehow moved beyond even Huard's understanding in the last few weeks—and he certainly should have known how very ordinarily human I was! Royalty, though, are often credited with more-than-human lustiness—perhaps he had attributed my coming to him to that cause.

While these thoughts were passing through my brain, Mennefer and Huard had cleared the table. Remembering my soaking clothing, I rose—time to slip back into the mundane world, high time! Huard rushed around to pull out my chair. I stepped away from the table, to find Mennefer kneeling at my feet. "Get up, child," I said. "You mustn't offer courtesies to which I have no right." But I had erred; I had used the diminutive sobriquet "child"—royalty used that name for lesser people for whom they felt some fondness.

Mennefer looked up into my face. "Eldrie, will you accept my oath? Will you take me for your liegewoman?"

"No," I said, as kindly as I could. "You don't understand the implications of such an oath. It would obligate me to care for you—and I have enough to do to care for myself."

"Please. I do understand. I want to serve you. Yesterday, in your presence, I had such a healing power as I have never had—the dragon flies on a sound wing today. And you held the dragons immobile with your will while lending me only a small part of your strength. Please accept my oath!"

Huard came and knelt beside her. "I am your liegeman, Eldrie Fitzroi. Allow me to add my plea to hers. When we leave here, I want to take her with us—she has become very dear to me. But she can't venture into a world she hardly knows and doesn't understand. Won't you grant her your protection and accept her service?"

I would have spurned her oath. I wanted none of it. I wanted to go back to what I had been. I wanted to laugh and joke in a tavern with friends who had no idea I had been sired by a king, and wouldn't have believed me if I told them. I wanted to flirt with all the men and take the one that made me laugh the most to bed with me, half-drunk and giggling in the dark. I wanted to bind up a child's cut and soothe an old lady's queasy tummy with a cup of mint tea. I did *not* want to go trailing about the world with an entourage, burdened with responsibilities and watched by critical eyes.

I would have spurned her oath. But I could not. I could not, any more than Huard could have disobeyed my voice of command or the dragons could have harmed us. I was beginning to have some inkling of the nature of Huard's "king's gift." It didn't reside in the royal personage, but in the followers. They invested it upon the object of their demanding loyalty and in so doing they were far more surely controlling than ruled. I could not spurn an oath offered in sincerity by a worthy person. I could not.

I reached out with infinite reluctance and laid my fingers against her forehead. She closed her eyes. "Mennefer, healing mage, give me your oath, then," I said sadly.

"I promise to serve and obey you in everything," she said breathlessly.

"Not everything, child," I corrected. "You say, 'in the practice of my craft and the service of my hand.' No liegewoman is expected to give up her personal rights."

"In the practice of my craft and the service of my hand," she repeated obediently. "Your commands will be as laws to me, and my loyalty, yours."

"I, Eldrie Fitzroi, accept your oath of fealty," I said. "From this day until we each and severally agree to end the obligation between us. For your service, I grant you my protection, and for your loyalty, my care." I let my fingers fall from her forehead and gave her my hand; she kissed the fingers.

"May I renew my oath?" Huard asked, holding out his sword. "The first was taken in haste. Accept my oath, Eldrie Fitzroi, offered after due consideration and freely."

I had just accepted Mennefer's; Huard had served me loyally (if not at all deferentially) for a much longer time. It would be a grave insult to refuse the oath now. I laid my hand on the hilt of his sword and offered him my hand to kiss when the ceremony was done.

"Now," I said, a little testily, "I have to go finish washing my clothes. With the permission of the civil and military branches of my government?" I nodded respectively toward Mennefer and Huard.

"I don't think you should wash your own clothes," Mennefer objected uncertainly.

"Whose should I wash, then?" Feeling a little better for having scored a hit, I went about my tasks.

It was now midsummer. Every afternoon, high thunderheads piled up and distant thunder grumbled in the mountains. Between my solicitous care and Mennefer's magic, Whitenose was sound again. It was time to leave. Once the summer rains began, the desert washes could flood without warning. Huard and Mennefer, still tender with each other and flushed with new love, stored the movable contents of her castle in deep inner chambers, while I packed up my medicines. We decided to load Whitenose only lightly; Huard's horse would have to carry most of what the pony usually carried as well as all of Mennefer's belongings—not, after all, a heavy load.

All our blankets were replaced with Mennefer's marvelously soft, thick, warm blankets and our bedrolls repacked. Good supplies of twice-baked ship's bread, dried fruits, other foodstuffs, and grain for the animals were made up into parcels and stowed in the packs where questing little pony noses couldn't get at them. Each of us carried a full canteen, and tight-woven water bags were slung on each pony and the horse.

As much as Mennefer looked forward to her new life with Huard, as curious as she was about the great world beyond her valley, still there must have been a pang in her heart as she stood in the entrance to the valley and looked back, gathering one last picture of her lifelong home to cherish. I saw a glitter in her eye. But the next moment she was striding confidently out, leading Graylegs with his pack of medicines, smiling bravely up at Huard.

For myself, beautiful as the valley was, I left it with a right good will. It had been a place of lonely torment for me. The future loomed ahead, as inescapable as the terrible trail that we had to climb to get out of this little paradise; I couldn't know what would happen, but I was full of foreboding. It would not be the future I thought I had chosen for myself. Even so, I was conscious of an uplift of spirits. Better to go boldly to meet what awaited than to wrestle darkly with phantasms from the cobwebby forgotten corners of my own heart.

"It isn't so bad going up," Mennefer said, looking up the trail. From below, it was almost invisible.

I looked up from my task, wrapping each hoof in leather boots. This was my idea; I thought it would give the animals more traction over that sloping precarious bulge in the cliff than their iron shoes, which were nearly worn out in any case. The boots need last only that far, and then it wouldn't matter if they wore through. "I hope not," I said. "I don't like the looks of that." I nodded at the blackish cloud that had boiled up earlier than usual today. Even as we all glanced at it, it was rent with sullen lightning.

"All done?" Huard said, straightening from his similar task beside his horse and dusting off his hands. "Then we'd better get going. Eldrie, you first with Whitenose. Then Mennefer and Graylegs. I'll follow with the horse. He isn't used to balancing a pack, and if he falls I don't want him taking anyone down with him."

I nodded and began my climb. "Don't come too close behind," I called. "Leave a little space for safety's sake. And move along smartly!" Then I was high enough to be out of sight and around the first switchback; I could no longer be heard and I bent my efforts to the climb.

Truly, it wasn't as bad going up. Even the bulge was beneath my feet before I realized it, and the leather boots on Whitenose's hooves clung to the rock as I had hoped they would. Once safely across, I paused and peered back and down, but only a few small sections of the trail on each level as it zigzagged back and forth across the face of the cliff were visible, and none of these were occupied by any living figures. The thunder muttered almost continuously now. I leaned into the climb again.

Some time later, as I paused to let Whitenose breathe, fat drops of rain began to splash down, one here, another over there. One struck me fair between the shoulder blades, a half-cup of water, icy still with the cold of the heights from which it had fallen. Whitenose shook himself vigorously as I gasped at the shock. I stepped to the edge of the trail and looked down. There was nothing to be seen; from the west, a curtain of rain advanced. Had Mennefer and Huard made it across the bulge of rock? If they didn't do so before the thunderstorm hit, they never would. The excess of empty air made me giddy and I stepped away from the edge.

Whitenose was nervously demanding to move on. Wise old fellow that he was, he knew what portended. I climbed on up the trail. There was nothing I could do to help my followers now. The rain was coming down more thickly, in stinging little lances. The temperature had dropped thirty degrees in the last half hour; it had still been blazingly hot when I crossed the bulge.

The rain increased, driving itself down upon Whitenose and me as if to sweep us from the trail. A gurgling stream was running down the cupped trail, and often I couldn't see where to put my feet to find a safe purchase. I was blinded, deafened, nearly suffocated by the force of the water, but still I pressed on, gasping. Half my attention was given to my own predicament, the other half to Mennefer and Huard, somewhere behind me. I had forgotten how much more of a walker I was than either, and how much better conditioned to physical effort. By how far had I outstripped them? Was I once again alone, with but a single pony? However much rancor I might feel for Huard's desertion, no matter how deep the jealousy I felt for Mennefer, I hoped desperately that they were safe and coming up the trail behind me. I certainly would never, even in my darkest moments, wish them to plunge to their deaths. I would play the princess for their amusement forever rather than that!

Almost without realizing it, I topped out, breathing heaving lungfuls of the intoxicatingly sweet rain-washed desert air. Whitenose and I were at the head of the trail, soaked and shivering, but safe. I found a place in the rocks nearby that was a little sheltered from the direct force of the rain, and set about searching for dry wood with which to build a fire. Surely they were close behind me and would appreciate a hot cup of tea with plenty of sugar in it when they arrived.

The summer rains in the desert fall with such overwhelming force that for a time they don't soak into the ground, but run off in violent rivers of a few hours' duration. By digging around the bases of the greasewood, I was able to find enough dry roots for a good fire, and soon I had water boiling and tea brewing. I huddled against the rock beside my fire, peering anxiously through the translucent curtains of falling water.

After a time, I drank a cup of tea myself. The rain was slackening now; the sudden thunderstorm was almost over. I gathered more wood and put it by the fire to dry. Suddenly Whitenose threw up his head and whinnied shrilly, and his greeting call was answered, not once, but twice! Over the rim of the cliff came Mennefer, soaked, bedraggled, her hair clinging to her cheeks in ropes, but smiling as she saw me and the fire. And there was Huard, close behind her, trudging wearily. I held out cups of tea as they came up, and they dropped gratefully to the ground beside the fire and accepted them.

"Look," I said, gesturing to the open gorge behind them. Spanning that airy chasm was a gleaming rainbow.

Chapter Ten

✤ ✤ ✤

WE WERE AMAZED to find a new landlord at the inn where we had stayed before; true, we had been gone some weeks, but Bennem and his wife had had an air of permanence about them. The mystery was explained shortly; as we sat down to supper (not up to the previous standard), the new innkeeper came up to Huard and spoke quietly in his ear. He excused himself and followed the man out.

Mennefer and I finished our meal and were sipping the thin dry wine of the country when Huard returned, followed by Bennem and a small, round, smiling woman. Huard's face was grave.

"Eldrie," he said, "Bennem and his wife Mallie are here to speak to you. Will you see them?"

I glanced suspiciously at him. He had better sense than to behave ceremoniously for no reason at all. Bennem and Mallie were almost clinging together with nervousness, bobbling shyly in the background as they waited for permission to speak. "Certainly," I said graciously.

"I was very sorry to miss them when we arrived this afternoon."

Bennem bowed as he came forward, beaming—not an innkeeper's professional smile, but a genuine smile of relief and delight. Mallie, a pretty, plump woman perhaps ten years my senior, dipped a graceful curtsy. "Your Highness," Bennem began.

"Please call me Eldrie," I interrupted. "I prefer it to my correct styling. And do, please, sit down and have a glass of wine, both of you."

Bennem gulped a little. "As you wish, Your—Eldrie." They sat gingerly at the table in what had once been their own inn and accepted the wine Huard poured for them.

"Why in the world did you sell this delightful inn?" I asked them. "In all my travels, and I have traveled all my life, I have never been made so comfortable, fed so well, or had cleaner, more cheerful surroundings."

"Thank you, Your—Eldrie. We felt that whatever we had to put our hand to, we ought to do the very best we could at it. But neither of our hearts were in it, if you know what I mean. And when you spoke about exploring far places and making maps, well, it struck a chord. For that's what we wanted to do. We stayed here for twenty years, and listened to the travelers' tales, and made our maps of imaginary lands, and all the while, our hearts were yearning to see those places ourselves. We figured that if we sold up and went with you, we could save a year or more getting started. And we aren't so young any more that we have a year to spare. I'm forty-six and Mallie's forty-three, though you wouldn't know it to look at her." He paused to twinkle at his wife, who blushed prettily. "So we sold the inn, and bought mules and an outfit, and we're ready to offer Your—you our oaths of allegiance and go with you now."

I stared at them, absolutely appalled. These poor deluded people had given up their livelihood and their comfortable lives, their drastic decision based on a few careless words I had let slip and Huard had accidentally confirmed. "But—but—what about you, Mallie? Do you really want to leave your home and go junketing around the known world and beyond?"

She raised her chin. "Oh, yes, I do!" she exclaimed. "It was I who insisted that we ask you if we could go with you now. I've always wanted to travel. With your permission, I know I could do a fine job of planning and supplying and outfitting the exploring parties."

"It's true," Bennem said proudly. "Her advice is sought by traders from all over these parts when it comes to planning trips. And she can outride and outwalk anyone I ever knew. She was born to be a caravan master."

I glanced dubiously at her comfortably round form. She saw the look. "Try me, Your Highness—er, Eldrie. On the trip back to your country, you see if I don't keep up and carry my share of the chores." The firm little chin came up again. "Come and look at the preparations I've made for this little trip and see if they aren't efficient."

"I'm sure they are," I said, capitulating to her determination.

"Then you will accept our oaths?" Bennem demanded. I saw their hands creep together and intertwine until the knuckles whitened. I had given these people a glimpse of an opportunity to realize their lifelong dreams. It was far more

important to them that I accept them than anything had ever been to me. The swearing of
oaths, the accepting of fealty and its reciprocal
responsibility, was a mere formality. They had
already committed themselves.

"I shall," I sighed. I stood, and they knelt before me and offered their allegiance, and—on
the same terms as I had accepted Mennefer, until it was mutually agreed to dissolve the oath—
I accepted their service. The rest of the patrons
of the inn watched in respectful silence until
the ceremony was over, and once it was concluded, a party commenced of its own accord.

I moved around the table until I sat with my
back to the wall and watched the merriment,
from which I was excluded by the status these
folk had endowed me with in their imagina-
tions. I was treated with every sign of deference
and respect; the finest bottle of wine in the
house was opened and placed before me with a
polished crystal glass; a tray of the finest nib-
bling foods the establishment could devise was
reserved for me alone to sample; and I was
stared at, whispered about, and left carefully to
my own exalted company. These folk had no
very clear idea of what a princess might do, but
they were positive that she didn't care to drink
the common wine, to laugh and talk with commoners, and certainly not to demean herself by
flirting with ordinary men, though many of
these were as attractive in their own way as
any I had seen and I would have liked to have
exchanged a little banter with some of them.

I saw Huard and Mennefer, each the center
of their own little circle of admiring listeners,
enjoying themselves hugely with their tales,
which (from the awed glances thrown my way)

were adding immeasurably to the catalog of my exploits. Huard was telling the greatly embellished story of our meeting; I was being portrayed as a positive mistress of swordplay, I was sure. Mennefer was relating how I had quelled the wrath of the dragons with a single glance. Occasionally Bennem or Mallie would lead up a little group of shy and mumbling people to present them. I had seen my father many times receiving these presentations, and he had always been gracious, kind, and smiling. Now I modeled my behavior on his. I even invited some of them to sit and talk, but they were uncomfortably tongue-tied and in mercy I soon had to let them go.

The party reached the point at which they would really set the rafters resounding with their merriment if I hadn't been present to cast a pall of respectability on the proceedings, and I judged it time to leave so they could enjoy themselves. I rose, and made my way toward the stairs, the assembled company opening out to make an aisle. I bade them a dignified goodnight, at which they all bowed, and went up to my room, accompanied by my entourage, having been, I supposed grumpily, magically deprived in the last two hours of the ability to put myself to bed without assistance. I did take advantage of the opportunity to ask Bennem to have the landlord send up another bottle of wine when they rejoined the merrymaking, and he fetched it himself. I was thoroughly drunk before the party downstairs broke up, though it didn't help me sleep. Nor alleviate my loneliness.

Mallie had indeed done an impressive job of preparing for the journey to wherever we were

going. I hadn't decided yet and the rest seemed
to believe that our goal was entirely my responsibility. Even Huard had given up urging me to
go back to Maritiene.

Bennem and Mallie had purchased four of the
spotted mules that were so useful for crossing
the desert. These were tough, enduring animals, with hard little hooves. Like all mules,
they were uncertain of temperament—they
seemed to hold their very existence against
their human owners, as well they might. But
these were well trained and in the shiny pink
of condition. Two were amblers, the easy-gaited
riding mules, and two were pack animals, of
the same stock but not gaited. The packs they
bore had been selected with great care to be
light, well-balanced, and complete, and all
equipment was of the very best quality, used
enough to be well broken in, but nowhere worn
or frayed. I inspected the contents of the packs
with delighted surprise. By some inspired
guess, Mallie had planned for five, and we
would travel in greater comfort and with more
convenience than I had ever managed before.
My two ponies would have nothing to carry but
my personal kit and my medicines.

Bennem and Mallie had their ambling mules.
Huard and Mennefer would ride the horse. This
left me to walk, leading the ponies, as I had
done for many years. I was content to have it
so. Not my entourage! They were scandalized
by the very idea.

"We'll just have to buy you a horse," Bennem
said firmly.

"I can walk," I insisted.

"It wouldn't be fitting," Mallie said.

"What would people think?" Huard added.

"And we'd all have to wait for you," contributed Mennefer.

"Allow me to assure you that you will not have to wait for me," I said. "Ask Huard. And anyway, I don't have enough money to buy a horse."

They traded glances among themselves. Having to deal with a liege lady who insisted upon being difficult was clearly wearing.

"Of course not," Mallie said comfortingly. "Who would expect royalty to carry money? Do you want to come and help me pick out a horse, or shall I choose one for you?"

"I'll pick out my own horse," I said, surrendering. It was becoming a little ridiculous even to me. Everyone in the party riding except for the liege lady? Even though I wasn't a princess, I was, by virtue of having all the others as my liegemen, the leader of the group. And I knew I didn't want a mule. It takes a special kind of person to deal with a mule's warped and devious outlook on life, and while I could establish rapport with almost any horse or pony, whether stallion, mare or gelding, a mule's motivations remained a mystery to me.

The horse dealer's pens were full of the spotted mules, the piebald jackasses that sired them, and the sturdy broodmares that were put to the jacks to produce them. There were few riding horses, and none of any quality. I looked over the lackadaisical specimens with marked lack of enthusiasm. They were jugheaded, green-broke, straight-shouldered creatures, guaranteed to jolt a rider's eyeteeth with every step and to go lame at every opportunity.

Mallie picked the best of a bad lot and began dickering with the trader. I lost interest and wandered off to have a look at the broodmares. And so I discovered, neglected and unkempt, a rare jewel, coated with the dust and manure of the broodmare pens.

It was her eye that caught my attention. It was an alert, intelligent eye, that looked across the backs of the larger broodmares at me with interest. Above it were two perky ears, the tips inclined inward until they were within an inch of touching. The face was wide between the eyes, slightly dished, with large, flaring nostrils on a tiny muzzle. The stringy mane graced a neck as curved and delicate as a swan's—and that was all I could see of her.

I ducked through the bars of the pen and made my way through the milling crowd of mares with their mule foals until I could see her whole. She was a dark, dappled gray, and though her legs were blemished with the scars of kicks from the other mares, they were basically as clean and straight as any I had ever seen. Her hooves needed attention badly—they were overgrown and cracked—but I could see that when properly trimmed, they would be of a good size for the size of the mare, dark and hard as flint, bell-shaped for greater resilience. Her back was short and broad across the loin. Her hip was long and almost level, the tail carried with high and jaunty pride above wide, well-muscled haunches. And those shoulders! That chest! The shoulders were laid back to an angle promising a long and enormously powerful, springy stride. The angle was reflected in the fetlock; her rider would hardly know when her feet hit the ground. And fast! I would have bet my virtue (had I still had any) that this mare could outrun and outlast any racehorse in my father's stables. And outmaneuver any war horse, into the bargain.

Why was this exquisite creature here among these nondescript broodmares? There was a weedy mule foal at her side—anyone could tell to look at her that a jack was no fit mate for her; why had she been so misused? What was wrong with her?

I approached her quietly and held out my hand. She sniffed it with curiosity, showing neither viciousness nor fear. It wasn't in temperament that she could be faulted, then. Nor in age; I estimated from her color that she was seven or eight, as dapple grays fade out until they're almost white by the time they're ten or so. A glance at her teeth verified my guess; the seven-year hook was present. Was she unsound? I ran my hands down her legs, which she lifted willingly, and found good flat bone, strong tendons, and large free-moving joints. She had a small splint on her right fore cannon, but no other flaws of conformation. Clapping my hands, I urged her into motion, and she moved square and true, with no nodding of the head. A hand run down her spine brought an expression of blissful pleasure, not a wince of pain. She was sound. And from the saddle marks, broke to ride, too.

I hurried back to Mallie, who was dickering spiritedly with the trader and, from the expression on his face, getting the better of him. "Mallie," I said urgently, "I don't want that gelding. I want one of the broodmares."

Both Mallie and the trader looked at me as if I had gone crazy. "Those mares aren't broke to ride," he said. "Now, this gelding is the best riding horse I've got, and I can get a pretty penny for him at the fall fair. But since Mallie's an old friend, I'll give you a special price."

"Will you sell me one of the mares?" I said insistently.

"Well, if you want, I guess," he said dubiously. "Which one did you have in mind?"

"The dapple gray with the star and stripe. In this pen over here. I'll show you."

I ducked into the pen and walked up to the mare, and she greeted me like an old friend. I put my hand on her neck and she followed me obediently to the gate, whickering to her long-eared son to follow. The trader was waiting with a halter, and I slipped it on her and led her out. The little mule hid bashfully behind his dam and peered out.

"I'm not one to run down my own stock," the trader said ruefully, "but that mare's just about useless. Some traders brought her in. They got her from a traveler who got her from some savage tribe away out to the west, clear on the other side of the desert, and from what they said, she was a long way from home even then. I never had a good foal from her; they're all as little and weedy as she is, and as hard to handle. She's broke to ride, but she's as touchy as a rattlesnake and as hard to sit on. You don't want this mare."

"If what you say is true, you ought to be glad to get rid of her, and at a reasonable price, too."

He shook his head. "If you were just anybody, I'd sell her to you and good riddance to a poor nag. But I've never sold a horse to a princess before. I want it to be the best one I've got. You can't ride this mare; she's dangerous."

"Get me a saddle and bridle that will fit her.

A bridle with a snaffle bit, mind; not one of those jaw-crackers you use on the mules."

"I've got the tack she was wearing when I bought her," he said slowly. "There's a snaffle on the bridle, too, come to think of it. I'll get it. It's the only saddle I've got with a high enough gullet for her withers." Mules tend to have almost no withers at all; the mare had good, prominent withers. The trader went away and presently returned, brushing at the dust on the most outlandish saddle I had ever seen. It was made of elaborately carved red leather, with a high, curved pommel and a padded cantle. The wide skirts had pouches built into them, and the stirrups were wooden and covered with a leather hood. There was a wide girth and a fringed breast collar. The bridle was similarly ornate, decorated with tassels of scarlet wool, and the bit, rusty as it was, was chased with thin inlays of silver. The thick saddle pad was woven of layers of the same scarlet wool that tasseled the bridle. We cleaned the gear as best we could, and I let the mare look the things over before I tacked her up.

She stood like a statue when I mounted and settled into the strange saddle. It felt different from any other saddle I had ever ridden; it held me in a forward position, and clearly the stirrups would have to be longer than I was used to. The trader lengthened them for me. I touched the mare with the calves of my leg, and she stepped out willingly and freely. With a second touch, she sprang into a gallop; either she had been taught never to trot or I hadn't given the correct signal. When I tightened the reins imperceptibly, she tucked her chin and slowed to a canter, and repeated signals brought only

slower and slower cantering, until she was lop-
ing almost in place. I loosened the reins and
she was gone like an arrow, so fast the wind
brought tears to my eyes. I wanted to lean forward over the withers as my masters had taught
me, but the saddle held me upright, swinging
loosely to her gait. I brought her to a walk once
more and touched her lightly on one side only;
she sidepassed across the field as easily and col-
lectedly as she had moved forward. A touch a
little farther back on her barrel, and she half-
passed diagonally; back farther yet and she
swung her hindquarters around her forehand.
A restraining hand on the bit and a touch in
front of the girth, and she pirouetted neatly on
her quarters. Truly, she was a marvel of training and sensitivity. No wonder these ham-
handed clods, used to muscling recalcitrant
mules about, had been unable to ride her.

The trader shook his head in amazement
when I rode up and dismounted. "I never would
have thought it," he exclaimed. "She's a mount
for royalty, right enough, and it will be my pleasure to give her to you. But I'll have to charge
you for the mule."

"I don't want the mule," I said, looking down
at the little fellow, who had scampered faith-
fully along with us, copying all his dam's ma-
neuvers. Just now, he was tucking into some
lunch, enormous ears flat along his neck.

"He's too young to wean," the trader said.
"And I might as well tell you, the mare's bred
back. I'm sorry, but I didn't know anyone would
want her for riding, and I thought she might as
well earn her keep. Do you still want her?"

I looked at the mule foal. He was too young,
all right, perhaps two months; if I insisted upon

separating him from his dam, he would die. And
the mare would be presenting me with just such
another next spring! But I had never ridden
such a horse. I had to have her! "Well," I said
reluctantly, "what do you want for him?"

He named a reasonable price, and Mallie immediately jumped into action, bargaining him
down and insisting upon the saddle and bridle
being thrown in for good measure. "And we
don't expect anything to be knocked off because
the mare's in foal," she added magnanimously.

The trader snorted. "I was going to give you
the tack anyway," he said with injured dignity,
"and I won't charge you a stud fee for the jack's
service. Fair enough?"

Mallie paid him. I wasn't paying attention; I
was gloating over the mare. Properly shod,
groomed, and grained up, she would be a fine
animal. I was going to enjoy riding her.

I did enjoy it when we rode out the next day.
I had worked lovingly over her the whole afternoon, and her gray coat gleamed, her mane and
tail rippled like a lady's hair. The farrier, having reshod all the other stock the day before,
had trimmed her chipped feet and shod her,
with me standing over him supervising, and
Bennem had polished the tack until it shone
richly red. There was a darker stain down the
left side of the pommel that no polishing would
remove—blood, I was sure. The blood of the
mare's owner and trainer. He or she had to be
dead. No one would willingly part with an animal so patiently and lovingly trained. The mare,
even with her ugly little son dangling at her
heels, was as royal among horses as my loyal
little following would have liked to have believed I was among people. She carried herself

with grace and dignity, nodding to the crowd
on the right and left as we rode out of town,
and the trader was there to cheer more loudly
than anybody.

We rode east. I had spent a long night doing
some thinking. I was now responsible for four
other souls and the thing they needed most was
a purpose in life. It seemed to me that Bennem's vision of exploring parties was what
we were best suited for. We were a hunter, a
healing mage, a caravan mistress, a cartographer, and a warrior (myself—I could think of
no other useful role that I could fill compe-
tently). We were mounted and equipped. Could
a better exploring party have been planned? But
such a party would need supplies, support, and
a home base—and I knew of no place to acquire
these other than in Maritiene.

Perhaps as Fitzroi I still had enough credibil-
ity with the merchant bankers there to arrange
funding for such an enterprise. There was
surely nowhere else that it was even feasible to
contemplate such a thing. None of the other
nations of the known world had the will or the
resources to mount such an expedition, and
certainly none where Eldrie Fitzroi was anything but a foreign physician. So it seemed that
Huard would have his way at last—I would go
home.

With a little simple discretion, my half-brothers
and other enemies at the palace would never
even know I was there. The princes I remembered would feel only contempt for the doings
of the merchant community. If we stayed at a
modest inn and avoided the places where the
court took their pleasures, there was no reason
anyone who might recognize me would ever see

me. I could even visit my mother with perfect safety. She had never been very important to me, nor seemed much concerned with what became of me, but she was my mother, after all.

There was only one difficulty with the plan, and that was Mennefer. If she weren't pregnant yet, she soon would be—in fact, I buried my head under my pillow and wrapped it around my head to muffle the giggles and sighs coming from the room next door even now. A pregnant girl couldn't be expected to undergo the hardships the members of an exploring expedition would have to endure. Indeed, we might well be gone for several years, which would mean traveling in unknown lands with a small baby.

I led the way when we started out, riding my beautiful mare, whom I had named Star, for the marking on her forehead, with the mule colt frisking about us. I had named him Rabbit—considering the neat ears his mother had, his were truly phenomenal. Huard and Mennefer followed, on Huard's horse. Bennem and Mallie, riding side by side on their ambling mules, brought up the rear, leading the two sumpter mules and the two ponies. I had thought this might cause difficulties, but the pack animals seemed to associate amiably enough.

So we rode east. I intended to follow the road only as far as the foothills, turning north along the old Traders' Road. It wound along west of the mountains, in the well-watered zone between the mountains and the Dry Plains. Bennem had several good maps of it. There were warnings of bandits and large predators, but it was surely preferable to following the road back through the forest and the mountains. Something truly fearsome lurked there, I knew, that Huard and I had barely escaped, though I couldn't remember exactly what. But I knew that I felt an unconquerable aversion to that road, and Huard confirmed that he did, too.

When I had traveled with Huard, or with Huard and Mennefer, I had done my fair share of the camp chores. Now that I was traveling with an entourage, I wasn't permitted to do anything more than care for my own horse, and that only by insisting upon it. While I bathed or washed up, camp was set up; I was given the best place to sit and a cup of tea to sip while the women bustled around preparing supper. Huard might hunt, if his divining charms gave promise of game; Bennem cared for the stock and then added to the map of our travels he was keeping. I stowed carefully in the bottom of my personal pack the canvas-bound casebook I had started as an apprentice and kept up ever since. I had a premonition that I would never again be allowed to be a practicing physician.

I would have been served first at meals, and allowed to eat in solitary state, but this I would not tolerate. I had often, in my days as a wandering herb doctor, bought a meal for some poor passerby so that I wouldn't have to eat alone, and it was foolish for the rest to eat cold food. And so I told them roundly. So we ate in the usual camp fashion, seated cross-legged around the perimeter of a canvas pack cover, the food in the center, discussing the travels of the day and plans for the morrow.

When the end of a day's travels brought us near one of the desert towns, we stayed at an inn, and I strictly enjoined everyone to keep my "rank" a secret. At one of these towns I purchased a long horseman's saber and a wooden lance. Star, I had discovered, was a war mare of the most exquisite degree of training, and the purpose of the high-pommeled saddle was more readily appreciated. It would have been almost impossible to fall out of it, even wounded, or (remembering the ominous stain) dead. Huard and I worked out a defensive strategy, he afoot, with his bow and claymore, I mounted, with lance and saber.

The Traders' Road was rough and wild. In most places it was no more than a winding track. There were isolated hamlets, but the people were sullen and shifty. There were good water and grass, though, and we made many miles every day. Day by day, Star and I became more of a team, more sensitive to each other, until I could guide her by the merest inclination of the head. It seemed at times as if there were some supernatural link between us. Poor little Rabbit took to spending his time with the ponies, who doted on him as elderly geldings will sometimes with foals, or with Mennefer, who felt sorry for the unwanted waif.

We had a few encounters with bandits. Our defensive strategy worked well enough that we were never really threatened, nor did we have to kill anyone. The sight of Huard, his great bow bent, and my lance leveled, war mare quivering with eagerness to charge but held in perfect check, was enough to discourage all but the boldest attackers. And the boldest had their minds changed for them by one lightning-fast charge and an arrow placed precisely at their feet.

Sneak thieves were a worse problem. We had to guard our goods and our stock constantly whenever we were near one of the towns. It was as well there were five of us.

At last we left the foothills behind and turned southeast through a gap in the mountain ranges. This would lead us along the southern border of Aurienne, just to the north of Termontaine, and so by way of smugglers' paths into the Forelt, familiar territory for me. We could have taken the northern branch of the road, through Aurienne; Lomel where the hairy half-men lived; and so into Nordron, Huard's home. But then the only way to Maritiene lay through the Salifer, the great salt marshes, and Adamar, my country's greatest enemy. I was not such a fool as to put a member of the royal family, even a bastard one, into the hands of the autarchs of Adamar.

It seemed that all the disadvantages of royal birth were mine. I could not go freely wherever I wanted to for fear that I might be seized and used against my country. I could not associate on easy terms with other people, not because I was too proud, but because they thought themselves too humble. Another disadvantage became apparent as I began to realize that I was alone among those who were in every way together. Huard and Mennefer, of course, were still in the first bloom of love, getting to know each other, adjusting to each other, exploring every nuance of newly awakened sensuality.

Bennem and Mallie had been wed to each other for nearly twenty years, and one might have thought they would have grown bored with each other in that time. One would have been wrong. They loved each other devotedly and with a simple, earthy directness that made their sharing of blankets not just a matter of habit and comfort but of frequent passion, as well. Often one pair would set the other off, and I would find myself surrounded by a veritable chorus of whispers and giggles and thrashing bedrolls. I gritted my teeth and spent a lot of time with my head under the rough pillow. I had never been so alone when I had no companions at all!

Nor had I ever been in such need of male companionship. I had of necessity spent long periods of time celibate. A healer's business often takes her into plague-ridden, famine-struck or war-torn lands where light dalliance is inappropriate or impossible. But there had also been times when I had had some warm, affectionate man to share my blankets. I had learned from each one, even those who had stayed with me a week or two and then decamped with a cheery admonition to take care of myself. Some, though, had stayed with me for months, and once I had lived with one for three years, and might have been with him yet if it hadn't been for—well, no point dwelling on dead history.

I had come to know and cherish these men, who had allowed me a share in their lives, though I had to admit that the partings were harder when I allowed myself to grow fond of them. Those were precious times, enchanted times outside the main business of life, the times when I had been briefly the half of a pair, and I had occasionally sought the opportunity for developing such a relationship when I felt the need.

And now I felt the need, not only sexual, though that need was present too, but emotional. I needed desperately to be touched and held and to touch and hold. I needed someone

to talk to, and someone who needed me to listen
to him. And there was no one for me. Mennefer
had Huard; Mallie had Bennem; and I buried
my head under my pillow.

Chapter Eleven

❖ ❖ ❖

THE FORELT! The secret, winding paths, each
known only to a certain band of smugglers! The
towns, perched like stairsteps upon the sides of
the mountains! The silent dark-clad people with
their sidelong, knowing smiles! I had spent
much of my early adulthood here. I knew this
place, these people. I had climbed these inter-
minable stairs, lived in that cottage under those
towering pines. I could call greetings to well-
remembered faces, and receive greetings in return. The clean, cool air smelled of resin and
smoke and dark ponies.

"Isn't there any flat land in the Forelt, that
the people must build up and down the cliffs?"
Huard asked, craning his neck to peer up a
street of stairs. We had left our stock at the inn
and were strolling about, stretching our legs
and enjoying the simple beauty of Three Pines,
the town. The folk of the Forelt don't believe in
crowding their neighbors, and native caution
commends them to keep their residences private, so each home is almost as isolated as if it
were in the midst of a forest, cunningly hidden
by boulders, trees, folds in the flanks of the

mountains. The visible parts of the towns are inns, shops, and public buildings.

"Not much flat land, and what there is, is needed for pastures." I laughed, taking a deep breath. "Besides, they like living perched on the sides of the mountains."

"What do they do for a living?" Mennefer asked innocently. "There don't seem to be any farms or workshops."

"Never ask a Foreltian that! Most of them are smugglers, and here you can buy goods from all over the known world, and never pay a cent of tax. But they're apt to suspect you of being an informer if you ask questions, and I daresay there isn't a man, woman, or child over the age of ten in Three Pines who wouldn't have his neck stretched in any of the civilized nations if their customs officers could only lay hands upon them. They say that the Forelt has no natural resources other than the cleverness of its people, and that's largely true."

"Look at the cloth in this shop!" Mennefer exclaimed. "And so cheap! Are these the true prices?"

"Only if you're willing to pay them," I chuckled. "Bargain a bit with the shopkeeper and you can get what you want for two-thirds the price. Less if you buy in quantity."

"We all could use some new clothes," she said, with a meaningful glance at my ragged garb.

"I'll come with you, sweet," Huard said, with a comically resigned sigh. "It'll save having to buy a donkey to get the stuff back to the inn." From the twinkle in his eye, he was looking forward to the shopping as much as she was. I remembered with a nostalgic twinge how he had enjoyed shopping in Termontaine; he should have the time of his life in this street of shops.

Mallie, Bennem, and I strolled back to the inn; the altitude here, coupled with all the steps we had to climb, made us short of breath. As we entered the lobby, Mallie remarked, "I believe I'll visit in the kitchen, just to see how they do things here. Why don't you two have a drink in the taproom?"

This was agreeable. I ordered a quart of the thick dark beer I remembered so well, and laughed to see the wine-drinking Bennem pull a face at the bitterness of the stuff. Presently the landlord came up. He had been talking with Mallie in the kitchen and had discovered that Bennem was a former innkeeper himself; they fell into conversation. Huard was coming in the door, laden with packages.

"Come back to my office," invited the Foreltian, "and I'll show you the booking system I've set up."

Bennem glanced up, saw Huard, and said to me, "Here's Huard and Mennefer coming back. Would you mind if I just have a look?"

"Of course not. Go ahead," I said, unable to imagine anything that would bore me more profoundly than an inn's booking system.

Huard stopped by my table, peering over the stack of bundles. "Hello, where are Bennem and Mallie?" he asked.

"Mallie stepped back to the kitchen for a moment or two, and Bennem's visiting with the innkeeper," I answered. "Where's Mennefer?"

"Oh," he chuckled, "she found a shop that sells furs and leather goods. I had about all I can carry so I'm dropping it by before she starts loading me up again. Will you be all right here by yourself?"

I sighed. "I've been all right by myself for the last sixteen years. It isn't I who's spending money like water. You'd better get back to Mennefer before we have to buy another pony to carry her stuff."

"True," he said. "And I saw a fur jerkin that I'm sure would fit me. I'll see you later, then."

He clattered up the stairs to our rooms and down again, waving as he went by the entrance to the taproom. I ordered another beer. A party of quiet, somberly clad young men came in on cat feet, drifting across the floor with a minimum of attention-catching movement, and took a shadowy table—a band of smugglers, resting between runs, or I missed my guess. I smiled to see them. What memories they brought back! I had honed my surgical skills patching up just such as they, after their clashes with the border guards.

One of them glanced at me, then glanced again. Presently he got up and approached my table. "Pardon," he said diffidently, "but aren't you a healer? Isn't your name Eldrie?"

"Yes," I said, mystified.

"I'm Dinel. You don't recognize me, I see," he said, smiling. "Likely enough you never noticed my face, but I reckon if you could see the other side of me, the memory might come back."

I peered more closely at him. "Oh, yes," I exclaimed. "I remember. I dug an iron arrowhead out of your—"

"Other side," he interrupted hastily.

I grinned. "Sit down, if you can," I invited. "How did it heal?"

He pulled up a chair. "I can sit just fine. I think it was the pat that did it."

I choked with suppressed mirth. He looked at me, and his eyes began to twinkle. Helplessly, we both broke into gales of laughter. He had been brought to me with a rather serious wound in the left cheek of his buttocks, nor had his companions made it any easier for him, with their teasing. He had been just my age, and boys of nineteen are often absurdly sensitive. He had complained feverishly of the pain; his friends had rallied him on being such a baby. I had chased them out with cutting words and given him a mild poppy draft, for he really had been in considerable distress, physical as well as emotional. I had dug out the arrowhead and stitched him up.

And then, because I felt sorry for him and because he really did have a cute little rear, I had patted him, on the right side, of course, and he had twisted himself around to look at me, and smiled through the tears of pain and the haze of the poppy draft. I had moved on the next morning and never seen him again, nor expected to, but I was glad that the wound had healed well.

He fetched his beer over from his friends' table, and when he returned, he slid in beside me on the bench. I looked into his face and smiled with pure joy. This was just exactly what I needed, a little attention, with the possibility of affection and a night or two together. There would be no commitments, no responsibility, and I would wake up some morning and find him gone—the smugglers could move like shadows when they wanted to, and I would never hear him go. When his arm crept around my shoulder as we talked of past times and old acquaintances and the times since we met last, and his other hand rested lightly on my knee, I moved a little closer to him.

Presently he leaned toward me, so that his breath tickled my ear. "It's going to be a long, cold night tonight," he said.

"It doesn't have to be," I said, letting my fingers trail over the back of the hand on my lap.

"No," he said, smiling deep in his dark eyes. "It might not be long enough."

A shadow loomed over us, and we both looked up. Huard stood there, looking grim and enormous, hand resting on the hilt of his claymore. Dinel drew hastily away from me. "Sorry," he said. "I didn't realize you were claimed." Looking up at Huard, he said apologetically, "No offense meant. I thought she was alone." He cast a reproachful glance at me, darted out from behind the table, and was gone. Huard watched him go, eyes narrowed.

I clenched my fists, almost choking with rage. I felt like a child whose proffered treat has been senselessly snatched away. I was humiliated by Huard's assumption that he had a right to censor my activities and by Dinel's perfectly justifiable conclusion that I had been ready to cheat on a husband or lover and had only been prevented from doing so by his unexpected return.

"I shouldn't have left you alone," Huard said conversationally, turning back to me. "I thought these smugglers would have more discretion . . ." Then he encountered my furious gaze and recoiled.

I couldn't trust myself to speak, or even to move. Mennefer came timidly up, piled with packages, and Huard hastened to take some of them and lead her away. When I had my breathing under control, I went up to my room, locked the door behind me, and went to the window, staring out into the gathering twilight.

There was a stirring next door, and a mutter of voices. I gasped with renewed rage. They were talking over what had happened, were they? Well, they were in for a shock in the morning, when they found me gone. Yes, I was leaving them for good. I couldn't stand it any more. It wasn't fair. It wasn't right. They had each other, and I had no one, and they dared to interfere when I tried to find someone, even only for a few nights of pleasure and companionship. And then they talked over my humiliation among them! I would take Star and the ponies and the colt and my medicines and gear and leave! And if they dared try to stop me, if they dared, if they so much as thought about it . . .

There was a timid tapping on the door. "Eldrie?" came Mallie's troubled voice. "Supper's ready, Eldrie."

I opened my mouth to tell her to go away, and found that I had no voice. My throat was closed as if clutched in strangling fingers. The tapping came again, more strongly. "Eldrie? Are you all right? Let me in, please, Eldrie." Then footsteps went clicking hurriedly away.

Bang! Bang! "Eldrie! Open the door!" It was Huard's voice. "Look, I'm sorry if you're upset. Let me in and we can talk about it."

Couldn't they understand that I just wanted to be alone? It certainly didn't bother them to leave me alone and lonely when I needed company desperately! Now that the only thing I wanted in the whole world was to be left alone, they came banging at the door. My lips formed the words, *go away*, but no sound came out. There was another confused stir outside, and the murmur of voices. A key rattled in the lock. There were disadvantages to having your companions chummy with the innkeepers.

The door opened slowly and Huard thrust his head in. "Eldrie? Are you all right?" I could see faces peering anxiously past him. Tiptoeing, they all came trooping nervously in, exclaiming to see me.

"Get out," I choked.

"Maybe the rest of you better go," Huard said grimly. "This is my fault. I'll talk to her." He closed the door behind them. "I don't understand why you're so angry," he said, reproachfully. "Mennefer has so many pretty things to show you, and you won't even see her. Mallie and the landlady fixed up an extra nice dinner, and you won't come and eat it."

There was nothing I could say to him. How could I say, you dumped me for Mennefer, and you two and Bennem and Mallie have been making love practically every night, and I'm lonely and I need a man, and I almost had a very nice one that I liked a lot and you scared him away? I couldn't say that. It sounded whiny and self-pitying. No real royalty would ever admit to such ignoble things.

"Listen," Huard tried again, "you might not think so, but we all care a lot about you and everyone's very hurt that you're acting this way. If you're mad, say so. What good do you think it does for you to refuse to speak to us?"

"It keeps me from murdering you," I said.

Huard managed to look relieved and startled

all at once. "But why?" he asked plaintively. "What did I do?"

"Look," I said, "none of this princess stuff was my idea. For once and for all, Huard, I am not a princess. I'm an ordinary woman, and I can't live like the four of you seem to want me to live. I get lonely. I have needs. How dare you interfere with me the way you just did?"

He stared. "Interfere? You mean you wanted that criminal to paw you all over the way he was doing?"

"If I hadn't wanted him to, he wouldn't have been doing it. Think back a minute, Huard."

"Well, yes," he said, dabbing reminiscently at his nose. "But, Eldrie, a common thug? A sneaking little border thief?"

"He's a smuggler, and a very uncommon one. And I knew him when I was young."

"All right, then, I'm sorry," Huard said, throwing up his hands and using a tone of voice that said he wasn't a bit sorry.

"Your apology is accepted," I said stiffly, in a tone that meant that I had no intention of forgiving him.

"All I can say is that he didn't stand up for himself very well. I don't care how long you knew him, he isn't worthy to—to—"

"Well, then," I spat, turning on him fiercely, "who is worthy? Just who the bloody hell is? And who gave you the right to make that judgment? Shall I trot every man that I want to take to bed past you for you to vet? You don't care if I'm alone for the rest of my life. Why should you? You have Mennefer. And Bennem and Mallie have each other. And who have I got? Tell me that, Huard. Who have I got?" To my infinite embarrassment, the tears I had been struggling so valiantly to master came bursting past my defenses and went straggling messily down my cheeks.

"So that's it. I see." He hesitated. "Eldrie, please believe me. It'll work out for you. I know it's tough right now, but you deserve better than—than one night with a taproom acquaintance. You'd be twice as lonely in the morning when he was gone, probably taking everything of value he could lay his hands on."

"Certainly I deserve better," I said with bitter sarcasm. "I'm a king's daughter. I deserve a prince in shining armor on a snow-white steed. Why didn't I think of that? And they're so easy come by, too. Just thick hereabouts. Go round up five or six and I'll pick one out."

"I didn't realize you were so unhappy," he said gently. "Let me go and talk to Mennefer. I'm sure she'll understand. I'll spend the night with you tonight."

"You will not," I said contemptuously. "Get out of here. And don't ever, ever interfere again, even if I pick out the lousiest beggar in the filthiest gutter in the known world. By all the gods of all the nations, if you're going to make a princess of me, then I'll act the princess. And that, my man, makes you just one of the peasants. Get out."

He left, closing the door gently behind him. I had scored a victory of sorts. At least I had certainly made him feel a great deal worse. Unfortunately, that didn't make me feel any better. Nor is it true that a good cry makes a woman feel better; it only makes her feel puffy and red-eyed and stuffy-nosed.

When I pulled myself together finally and went down to see about supper, the others had already eaten. But they cleared away the crumbs and set the best meal they could scratch together before me. The rest watched me eat, pathetically anxious that I should enjoy my food. It all tasted like dust. But I sent Mallie back to the kitchen with a compliment for the cook, anyway, and made myself sit with them sipping hot ale with spiced baked apples floating in the bowl. But it didn't work. Everyone was strained and stiff and the tears kept starting to my eyes again.

The next morning Mennefer and Mallie were busy with their purchases of the day before, making up the cloth into garments and packing things, with Bennem helping them. I delved into my purse and counted what I had left over from selling the botanicals in the Termontaine—not much.

"What are you doing?" Huard inquired curiously, when he found me rummaging in the pack that Graylegs usually carried.

"Well, I wanted to do a little shopping too, and I don't have enough money, so I thought I'd sell a few of these medicines at the apothecary shop. It doesn't much look like I'm going to need them," I added. My intention to run away from my responsibilities had evaporated overnight. Not only was it not the right thing to do, it probably wouldn't even work. They'd just follow me, and with Huard's superb tracking skills, it wouldn't be long before they found me.

"You can't do that. Anyway, you should have plenty of money. Let's see."

I handed him the purse. "Four hundred and twenty-two and six tenths of that is yours," I explained. "Twelve and nine tenths is mine."

"I don't mind if you use mine."

"I mind."

He sighed. I was being difficult again. "Then declare a head tax. You announced that you were the princess and I was the peasant. Isn't that what princesses keep peasants for? Paying taxes?"

I felt the tears prickle up to the surface again and turned my head so that he couldn't see. "I'd rather sell the medicines. You're a married man now, Huard, and likely to be a father before long. Four hundred and twenty-two is a lot of money and a man with a family has to think of these things. In fact, count out my twelve and nine tenths and keep the rest. I don't want to do it anymore."

"Don't worry about supporting my family. Please take the money. I have plenty."

I shook my head stubbornly and went on sorting out the medicines. He sighed again, but picked up the bundle and carried it for me to the apothecary shop, were I got a good price for some of the more exotic plants and pocketed eighty-two and three tenths when the bargaining was done. Added to my twelve, this made a respectable amount for shopping, enough to buy a sturdy new suit of clothes, some boots, and a pair of gloves, if one chose carefully. I wandered up and down the center of town, looking in the shop windows. I couldn't find anything I wanted to buy, at a price I could afford to pay, though, and we returned to the inn at noon empty-handed.

The women and Benñem went back to their work after lunch, and I went shopping again. This time I found a pair of gloves I liked, which I let Huard carry for me, since he insisted upon trailing me around. I also bought a sugar cake in a bakery—once I had been very fond of them, but my tastes had changed.

The next morning I discovered what project it was that had kept everyone so busy—it was a new riding suit for me, charcoal gray trimmed with black and crimson to match Star and her tack. They had bought a hat, cloak, and boots to match, too. I was touched by the gesture. I had been making things very difficult for everyone the last few days, and while they had been making things difficult for me, they at least had not done so on purpose.

"Thank you," I said, pirouetting so they could see the magnificence they had created. "Thank you all." I looked at my reflection in the window at the front of the inn and sighed internally. The splendid woman in the glass was not a woman to be desired. A woman of consequence, no doubt, and one to be reckoned with. Not one to laugh in the dark with. Whether wittingly or no, they would keep me from choosing the scruffiest beggar in town or anyone else. I might as well resign myself to lonely chastity.

From the Forelt the road drops steeply into Maritiene (the official road—the smugglers' trails are another matter). We crossed the border at the opposite side of the country from Maritiene City on Mari Bay. Not being smugglers, we were stopped by the customs officials, who were brisk, polite, and efficient. We paid the entry tax for my four followers. "I'm a citizen of Maritiene," I declared.

"Name, date, and place of birth?" the man inquired.

"Eldrie Fitzroi, the third year of the present reign, Maritiene City," I said.

The man looked up, startled (very nice blue

eyes). He knew the meaning of the term Fitzroi.
But he wrote it dutifully down, after peering
into my face. "Occupation and reason for
travel?" he asked.

"Physician. And traveling in the practice of
my craft."

"I see. Welcome home, Eldrie Fitzroi. I hope
you'll be staying with us for good this time. If
there's anything I can do to expedite your trip
to the city, please call on me."

It was my turn to be startled. If I had thought
I would be believed, I wouldn't have laid claim
to my name. I had done so mainly to demon-
strate to Huard that I was not a person of consequence in my own land. And I certainly hadn't
expected to be called by an honorific. "Thank
you," I said feebly. "I think we can manage on
our own. But it's very kind of you to offer."

He came out from behind the counter to bow
as we left. "I don't think we'd better tell anyone
else who I am," I told my party as we mounted
up. "I certainly didn't expect that reaction."

There was no sense of homecoming. I had felt
more at home in the desert, and infinitely more
comfortable in the Forelt. Here, I was in enemy
territory and I moved with the wariness of a
hunted deer. Huard or Bennem dealt with innkeepers and others and never gave my name,
and most nights I ate in my room, avoiding the
taprooms for fear of being recognized. The customs official had severely shaken my blithe confidence that sixteen years had granted me
virtual anonymity.

Unobtrusiveness wasn't made any easier to
attain by my four retainers. They had bought
the cloth for, and sewed as we traveled, suits of
the same gray cloth trimmed in crimson that I

wore, though of a simpler pattern. These they
donned with such pride that although I fumed,
I hadn't the heart to force them back into their
shabby old clothes. But there was no doubt that
it had the look of livery. It was certain that the
folk of the rich farming areas through which
we passed and of the towns in which we stayed
were convinced that some personage had come
their way, even if they weren't sure who.

These broad cultivated acres through which
we rode, the busy craftsmen's workshops in
every town, and the lively commerce that
thronged the highways and rivers, was the
source of Maritiene's wealth and power. My
brothers were very wrong to scorn the merchant enterprises. My father knew this, and had
encouraged the growth and development of
cash-crop agriculture, the crafts, and trade. The
queen, on the other hand, was of the old aris-
tocracy that based its wealth on the land and
the cheap labor of ignorant tenant farmers.
These turned up their noses at honest work and
at money that was earned rather than inher-
ited. To them, there was only one fit trade for
even the most impoverished sprout of a noble
family—the military. My brothers had learned
this attitude at their mother's knee, so to speak,
while my mother was of the merchant class
herself.

Maritiene was not a first-class military power,
I knew. Its subsidized the merchant marine to
arm and defend its own ships and maintained
an adequate army to defend its borders, neither
strong enough to embark on any wars of con-
quest. Adamar to the north peered across our
common border and licked wolfish chops at the
tender prey of Maritiene, but although the au-

tarchs maintained a huge army, it was an ill-equipped, half-starved, usually unpaid rabble in no condition to match the much smaller but highly professional and completely up-to-date force that my father stationed along the northern border.

The prince-bishop on the south would also have dearly liked to have dipped into the wealth of Maritiene, but, having no decent harbor anywhere on his coast and therefore no navy to speak of, was obliged to consider what any forays across the border would cost him in the way of raids from the sea. His people, hampered in their agriculture by poor soil and resolutely conservative farmers, were also greatly dependent upon the farms of Maritiene for food, and an embargo on exports would have brought him to his knees in short order.

The Forelt was no problem, except to the customs service, and the people of gloomy Winterholt had all they could do to survive from one year to the next. They were a nuisance only, raiding across the border for enough food to fill the empty bellies of their children, too weak from semi-starvation to do more. If I had been my father, I would have seen to it that their sufferings were alleviated and thus secured that section of my border; but I wasn't my father and doubtless he had his reasons for acting as he did.

Better that these should be my older brother's problems than mine; the king of Maritiene was a juggler perpetually on stage, balancing all these factors and more to keep the nation on a smooth course. No wonder my father had been always tired! But I hoped my brother had grown and matured since last I saw him.

It was a shock to me when I discovered that my older brother was dead. I had certainly never been fond of him. On a personal level, he had been a braggart and a bully and stupid into the bargain. But he had been the heir to the throne and I had thought (without really thinking about it) that he was immune to the accidents that befell ordinary folk.

We had paused in one of the river's ports for the first day of the Harvest Festival, and were enjoying the music and dancing in the public square, when I happened to glance up and see the pictures displayed on the front hall. "That's Felan!" I exclaimed, focusing on the picture to the left of King Eldran's. "Why isn't Jovian's picture up there?"

"Eh?" said Bennem, who happened to be standing next to me.

"That's Felan's picture, my younger—er, the younger prince. Sir, excuse me, why is this picture up there of Prince Felan instead of Prince Jovian?" I laid my hand on the arm of a laughing young man in the costume of a prosperous farmer.

He looked me up and down—I was wearing the green gown in honor of the occasion and I would have enjoyed the appreciation in his glance under better circumstances. But he sobered. "Didn't you know? Prince Jovian was killed in a hunting accident, oh, must be three years ago now. No, two. So Prince Felan is the heir. Say, lady, are you all right?" He took my arm solicitously; I must have turned pale.

In truth, I felt profoundly shocked. I should have heard about this. "I thank you, sir, it came as a bit of a surprise to me. I've been out of the country for some time. But I'm fine."

"Well, it's not a completely bad thing," the young farmer said, slipping an arm around my waist. "Prince Felan is a bit of a sissy, but Jovian was downright mean, a real demon's-child, from what I hear. Come over to the refreshment tent, pretty lady, and I'll buy you a cup of tea and tell you what I know about it."

I slipped out of his hold. "Thank you for the thought, lad, but I have to keep an eye on my son over there. He tends to lose his head over the most unsuitable girls." I pointed out Huard, who was studying the gimcrack contents of a booth selling trinkets for fairings with savage concentration.

The young farmer looked at me, looked at Huard, and then back at me. A slow grin spread over his face. He wasn't stupid, that one. "I understand, pretty lady. Better keep an eye on your grandson, too." He pointed to Bennem, who was watching us anxiously. With a cheery salute, he melted back into the crowd. I watched him go with definite regret.

"I wasn't interfering," Huard said.

I sighed. "No. But this was different."

Huard scratched his head. "I don't understand. You pitched a fit when I chased away a smuggler, a common criminal who will doubtless end his career on a gallows. That young man was respectable, clean, neat, polite, and probably kind and considerate."

"Intelligent, too," I agreed. "He had a nice smile, he wasn't married, and he has a fine future in store managing his own farm. He's doubtless a rising young member of the local grange, and if he isn't an accomplished lover, he could easily be taught to be."

"Well, then, why—"

"We're in Maritiene. An affair with that estimable young man could destroy his promising future and embarrass my father. Think about it. Ordinary farmer takes the king's daughter for his mistress. Word of it gets out. Other farmers are bitterly jealous; he loses his influence in the grange. The girls he should be courting give up on him, knowing they can't compete with what they perceive as rank and power. People start whispering—did you hear about Eldrie Fitzroi? She's bedded a farmer upcountry. No, three farmers. Ten farmers and three river boatmen. Eldrie Fitzroi can be had by anything in pants. And so on. And what good could come of it? None for him, none for me, none for the country."

"Oh." There was a long silence. "And even if anyone had found out about the smuggler, no one would have believed it."

"In the Forelt, I'm just Eldrie the physician. They've never made the connection between the healer and the Fitzroi—why should they? And those smugglers never ask questions and they never tell anyone anything."

"Oh. I see. I'm sorry. I didn't understand." This time there was genuine contrition in his voice. The rest of our party had gathered up and we moved off toward the game booths.

"Let it go, Huard. This is the Harvest Festival. We're going to have a good time whether anyone wants to or not. There, a ring toss. Who can throw the rings over the pegs and win a prize?"

The rest moved eagerly to the booths, and soon were absorbed in the games, spending money and laughing with delight when they won. Huard, his arms loaded with tawdry ornaments, toys, and gewgaws, strolled along with me. Evidently he had no taste for the games either. "I always thought that royalty could do anything they want. That's not so, is it?"

"In a way, it is. No one can stop a king from doing as he pleases, if he's utterly careless of the consequences of his actions. That's the situation in the Protectorate. The Protector is an egomaniac. He acts only for the immediate gratification of his own whims, not for the good of his country. But consider what a state the Protectorate is in!"

"I see what you mean," Huard agreed ruefully.

"The trouble is, the actions of royalty have more drastic consequences than the actions of ordinary folk. Compare what might have happened if I had crawled into that farmer's bed with what would happen if, say, Mennefer had done the same thing. You'd have been hurt, probably your relationship would have been damaged, the five of us might have been upset, but there would have been no lasting effects on any but the personal level. True royalty has to take all these things into consideration. I'm glad I'm not a real princess; letting him put an arm around my waist might well have precipitated a disastrous war! I won't breathe easily again until we're safely out of Maritiene."

"I begin to see why you didn't want to come home."

"You can be grateful you won't find out even more personally."

"What do you mean?"

"Well, suppose I did go to the palace and claim whatever position I have. As my liegemen, you'd all go with me; it's my right to have people of my own about me, though for a bastard, four would be straining the privilege a bit. But then it would be you who would be watched, and whispered over and gossiped about. That would do you no harm, not unless you cared about the harm it was doing me! And you'd be the target of intrigues to discredit you, and through you, me. You'd be offered bribes to use your supposed influence with me to forward someone's schemes. You'd be blackmailed and harassed and made the butt of cruel jokes. As I said, be grateful. We won't go anywhere near the court. We'll only meet the merchant bankers, who are businesslike people. If they turn us down, it'll be because they honestly don't see the opportunity for a profit commensurate with the risk, not because they're maneuvering for an advantage in some game of prestige and power."

Huard grinned ruefully. "And from all this, you ran away just as soon as you could possibly make it on your own."

"Something like that. I didn't escape uncorrupted, though."

"You did," he said, taking my hand. "I've always been proud to be your liegeman. How could anyone be proud to serve a corrupt liege lady?"

I only shook my head. My heart was full of the knowledge of my own evil, but I couldn't explain it to Huard. I *knew* what might happen to the lover of the king's daughter, here in the king's own lands; had I not thoughtlessly destroyed my only friend Janni by just those means, in spite of his pleading with me to leave him alone? And he hadn't even been my real lover.

Chapter Twelve

✤ ✤ ✤

I CHOSE THE INN we were to patronize carefully.
It was a large one, comfortable but not luxurious, on the outskirts of Maritiene City. It was a
favorite of the owners of small transport companies and their riverboat captains and wagon
masters; there was a lot of coming and going,
plenty of accommodation for stock, and many
large parties staying there at any one time. On
the other hand, it was famous neither for its
cuisine, which was good but not distinguished,
nor for the entertainment available. We would
go unnoticed here, nor was there much chance
of meeting anyone from the palace.

Bennem went into the innkeeper's office to
dicker over the price of lodgings. I went out to
tell Huard to turn the horses over to the hostlers and bring our packs in. I was surprised to
see him handing something to one of the boys
who always hung about the courtyards of inns
waiting for odd jobs and messages to deliver.
The boy looked up at him, wide-eyed and open-
mouthed.

"Get along with you, quick, run," Huard said,
shooing the boy out of the gate.

"Where in the world were you sending the
boy?" I asked, as I came up to him. "I didn't
know you knew anybody in Maritiene City."

He jumped as if startled. "Er—I've visited
here before, you know," he said tightly. "I was
just sending a message to an old friend to let
him know I was in town."

I surveyed him. There was something odd in
this. "I would have been happy to let you go

visit him in person," I said. "I hardly think I've been such a harsh taskmaster as all that."

"No, of course you haven't," he said. "But I wanted to stay with you. He can come visit me when he has time."

"Something certainly did surprise the messenger," I commented. "I hope you didn't tell him who I am."

"Of course not. I expect the boy had given up hope of a job for the day, that's all."

He was lying to me again. But why? I could see absolutely no reason for him to deceive me. I looked into his face, but there was nothing but the most limpid candor in his clear blue eyes.

"Hm," I said dubiously. "Well, we have a suite of three rooms and a parlor for two weeks. If we haven't arranged financing by then we might as well forget it. Get a couple of porters and take all our gear up to the rooms, if you would. We'll change clothes. I need to look as important and prosperous as I can when I visit the banks. We'll have a bite of lunch and then we might as well start making the rounds of the bankers' counting houses."

After considerable hesitation, I chose the gray riding suit, though I strictly forbade the others to wear their matching gray livery. "I want to look prosperous," I told them, "but I certainly don't want to attract the attention of the palace."

"Isn't the gray a little casual for city wear? I think you should wear your red brocade," Mallie objected.

"Not in the daytime. I should wear a walking dress in a conservative color for this kind of business. But at least I look like an explorer, if not a businesswoman."

"You're going to have to tell the bankers who you are," Bennem said. "Your name is about the only asset you've got. You should dress the part of a king's daughter."

"How about one of the silk blouses and linen skirts?" Huard suggested.

"If I had a jacket and a hat to match, that would be good," I conceded.

"We'll have to stop at a clothing shop and a milliner's on the way and buy you a jacket and a hat, then," Huard said.

"I guess I can wear the primrose and buy a gray jacket," I mused. "All right. Mallie, would you mind buttoning me up?"

I was annoyed to discover that they had apparently interpreted my change of plans as permission to wear their gray livery when I came down to the dining room. I was even more annoyed when they all stood gravely and waited for me to take my place at the head of the table; people were staring. Half the staff of the inn was lined up to serve my party, having discovered who I was, or at least that I was somebody, and the elegant bows my people offered me as I approached didn't do anything to reduce the gawking delight with which I was being regarded.

"What do you think you're doing?" I hissed, as I was helped ceremoniously to a chair.

"You don't think the bankers will inquire at the inn where you're staying?" Huard asked.

"I don't care if they do, damn it. I tell you, I'm in danger every minute I'm in Maritiene, and twice as much here in the city. I thought you understood."

"Believe me, I understand," Huard said. There was a note in his voice that startled me and I looked sharply at him, but his head was bent over a platter that was being offered him and I couldn't see his face.

There was a clatter in the courtyard of the inn—a sizable party arriving with carriages and on horseback, evidently. There was stamping and excited shouting. Slowly I put my napkin aside and looked at Huard. He wasn't eating. Mennefer was looking from him to me with dilated eyes.

The message he sent this morning. Indeed, the messages he had sent from every inn we stayed at. The determination with which he had stayed with me, no matter how I tried to free him. The ease with which he had believed my preposterous story of being a king's daughter. The innumerable times he had tried to talk me into coming home. This Huard was no simple hunter. He was a Hunter, and I was his prey. With what infinite patience, with what immeasurable persistence, he had stalked me! With what cunning wiles he had deceived me! And at last, as it was said that the Hunters always did, he had brought in his quarry.

I rose and stepped from behind the table. It was too late to flee; the doors of the dining room were even now being flung wide and all the brilliance and color of the court was flooding through them. In the center of the crowd, more brilliant than all the rest, my brother Felan stood, removing his embroidered gloves with finicky care.

I dropped a profound curtsy, being dressed in skirts, and Felan moved forward to take my hand in his. "My dear sister!" he said in his clear tenor. "Eldrie, my dear! Welcome home,

Eldrie! We've been searching for you for so long!" He squeezed my hands so tightly it hurt.

"Your Highness," I murmured. "My condolences on the loss of your brother. I only heard yesterday."

"You always used to call me Felan, when we were children together," he said. "Please call me that now. My dearest sister—almost my twin! Do you think I want honorifics from you?"

I gave him a startled look. True, we had been raised almost in the same cradle; there was only two months difference in our ages. In spite of that we had never been very close—rivals, rather. Yet there were actual tears in his eyes, and his hands that clutched mine were trembling. "As you wish, Felan," I said. "Are you well?"

"As well as I can be, with all—but there'll be time for this. Come to the palace. As soon as we knew the Hunter had found you, a suite was prepared for you."

I cast a bitter look at Huard, who didn't raise his eyes to mine. "I don't wish to return to the palace, Felan. There's nothing for me there, and nothing I can do to help anyone. Please just let me go."

"Oh, Eldrie," he whispered in anguish, "can you ever forgive me? I'll never forgive myself—there hasn't been a single day since you left that I haven't blamed myself."

To say that I was astounded was to say that the great ocean was damp. "Forgive you for what?" I asked blankly.

"For driving you away, and for all the terrible things that have happened to you since you left, and for—for—but come, Father's waiting. The carriage is outside. Your people can bring

your belongings." He was pulling me toward
the door, still holding me by my two hands.
"Never say you aren't needed. Father needs you.
I need you. Come, Eldrie, please." He was tug-
ging me outside, where footmen in the royal
livery were holding open the door of a coach.

If I set foot in that carriage, I was lost. I believed not one word of anything Felan had
said—he had always loved to bait me. Franti-
cally I tried to free my hands from his grasp,
but he was stronger than when I had left.

"Allow me to assist you, Eldrie Fitzroi,"
Huard said from behind me, and I was picked
up effortlessly and deposited inside. Felan
scrambled in after me.

"Damn your soul to hell, you sneaking, lying,
cowardly traitor," I gritted at Huard. The carriage started off with a lurch.

"Bring your things and your animals to the
palace," Felan shouted out the window. Settling back beside me, he turned to look at me,
taking my hand again. "Why didn't you ever
come back?" he asked. "Or even write to tell us
where you were?"

I sighed, defeated. I was caught, fair and true
and by my own foolish carelessness. "I didn't
think anyone cared where I was," I said. "And
I didn't come back because I wasn't needed
here."

"It was I who told you that," he said. "And I
was lying. You were everyone's favorite, you
know. Jovian hated you because Father loved
you best of any of us, and I was too much of a
coward to defend you from him. Oh, Eldrie, you
should have known I was lying! If only you
could have waited until I was strong enough, I
would have protected you from Jovian!"

This statement was patently absurd. Jovian had always been strong for his age, and, like the demon's-child he had been named, he enjoyed hurting people. Felan even now was no taller than I, and probably not as heavy. He had always preferred subtle barbs to physical blows. I could make no sense of his sudden protestations of concern.

"Felan," I said slowly, "I have never blamed you for anything—except the poem about the stable boy—and I didn't leave because of anything you said."

He flinched. "I did write the poem," he confessed. "I was so jealous! But I never meant anyone to read it."

"Jealous?"

"Jealous that you had someone to love you," he explained. "It seemed so unfair. Father loved you best, Jovian had already had two or three of the maids, Mother had Uncle Joss. I had no one. So I made up that poem. I knew it wasn't true."

"Well," I said wearily, "it's all long past and over with. I'll forgive you the poem and you forgive me for running away. What does Father want me for, do you know?"

"I'd better let him tell you that," Felan said. The carriage rumbled through the palace gates—the family entrance, I noted, not the public one. They clashed shut behind us with a sound like prison bars closing forever. I shuddered.

"Do you hate coming back to us so much, then?" Felan asked wistfully. "Was it really so terrible here?"

"Of course not. But I don't like living here. I hate the lying and the intrigue and the politics and never telling people to their face what you think of them. I loathe never being allowed to do anything useful."

"It must have been worse, though, living as a commoner, working for a living. You must have been cold and hungry and lonely. You must have been in danger often."

"It wasn't that bad, Felan. I was usually warm and well-fed and with company that cared about me, not what advantage they might gain from cultivating me. And when I was in danger, I could take care of myself."

He gave me a look half-envious and half-admiring. "Father used to say proudly that you were the best man of us all, when you'd ridden a horse neither of us dared go near or beaten us once again at fencing practice or taken one of Jovian's beatings without a whimper. I used to cry when he hit me."

The footmen opened the door and Felan jumped out, as lithe and active as ever. It had been foolish of our father to speak in the boys' hearing, I thought. Felan could have been a notable athlete—a gymnast, perhaps—if he hadn't been discouraged with comparisons.

Felan conducted me to a room near the public reception room in the royal quarters and sent a message to the king to let him know I was here. I was prepared to wait patiently, but only a few minutes passed before the door banged open. I leaped to my feet and started to curtsy, only to be swept into a hug. "Eldrie. Eldrie. Eldrie," my father was saying, over and over. I was held at arm's length and inspected. "You look so well! Felan, go and tell your mother that Eldrie's here."

"Your Majesty," I began, tremulously. "Father?" He looked like himself, tall, virile, commanding. In the brown hair (shot with gray, now), the eyes, the strong nose and square chin—I was looking in a mirror that showed me an older, masculine form of myself. I had forgotten how much we were alike.

"Eldrie, my little pet. I'm so glad you're back."

"I'm sorry about Jovian—the grief his death must have caused you."

"I wasn't a very good father," he said ruefully. "I let his mother spoil him and Felan. I let you be driven away."

I spoke to him as I never would have dared speak to the king before, encouraged by his affectionate reception. "It was better for me to leave. There was nothing for me to do here. For that matter, there's nothing for me to do now. Wouldn't it have been better just to let me go my way?"

"Eldrie, my dear child, there are so many, many things you can do. Maritiene needs you. The international tensions—the economic problems—I understand that you would rather be free of these obligations. As would I! But of all my children you are the one I trust the most. You have the royal gifts, Eldrie. Felan doesn't, and Jovian didn't, but you always did. I need you!"

"So you set a Hunter on me to bring me back?" I asked. I bore a grudge about that.

"Twenty Hunters. I needed you so much! The political situation—and Jovian dying—your place was here. I knew that if I could just explain to you, you'd understand. After all, you have the royal gifts, and they aren't lightly escaped."

"Evidently not," I said wryly.

"Here's the queen now," the king said, turning as the door opened. Queen Amalie came sailing through, her everpresent friend Joss in the background.

"Eldrie, my child!" she said, coming forward and catching me as I started to curtsy. She kissed me dryly on the cheek. "How good it is to have you home!"

"Your Majesty," I murmured. "How nice to see you so well and happy. And Uncle Joss. It's good to see you again, too," I added. I had almost forgotten how the queen's lover used to play with us when we were children. He was the only one who had treated us with humorous and affectionate impartiality, and we all four used to climb on his lap for the marvelous stories he told. In fact, a lot of the fairy stories I loved so well I had first heard from Uncle Joss. I had only begun to hate him when I understood the wrong he had done my father, when I was twelve or thirteen—and even then, I hadn't liked hating him. He smiled and bowed.

"Eldrie Fitzroi," he said. "We all missed you."

"I must go," the king said. "There are forty people waiting to see me. Eldrie, you'll have dinner with Felan and me tonight and we can get to know one another again."

"Of course, Your Majesty," I said, sweeping a curtsy as he headed for the door.

"Eldrie, my dear, you'll spend some time with me tomorrow, won't you?" the queen said warmly. "I'll want to hear all about your adventures." She gave my skirt and blouse a quizzical look; they were new and (for an itinerant herbalist) very fine, but seen through the queen's eyes, they were plain and quaint. "I'll have all the best dressmakers in. You'll need a whole wardrobe, I'm sure."

I curtsied again. "I'm at Your Majesty's disposal," I said. This was certainly true, and it did no harm to let her know that I knew it. I couldn't afford to alienate her any further than she no doubt already had been by having been forced to acknowledge me as her husband's daughter. But Uncle Joss winked at me as they left.

They had given me a suite of apartments within the royal quarters, although of course not those where Thildie had lived for such a short and closely supervised time between coming of age and marriage. These were farther from the king's suite. They had been newly decorated, though, and someone had gone to some effort to make me feel at home there. The sixteen-year-old Eldrie would have loved them. They had been done over in golds and russets, with an equestrian theme in the paintings and knickknacks. Well, it was better than the pink and white and insipid flower paintings with which the princess's apartment was decorated!

There were ample accommodations for my party, as well as the complete staff of butler, housekeeper, cook, dresser, maids, and footmen that had been provided. Huard, Mennefer, Bennem, and Mallie would rank as retainers, rather than servants, and would eat with me on ordinary occasions. When we ate in the Grand Salon with the king I would be seated at the royal table, though not within the central area reserved for the Family, and they would be accommodated among the professional folk—accountants, physicians, secretaries, civil servants, such raffle and scaffle. I hated it already.

Rank, privilege, ceremony, protocol, procedures, etiquette, were closing on me like a troop of gloating enemies.

Presently my four liegemen arrived, escorted by a train of servants carrying our baggage, whom the butler led on to the quarters the housekeeper had chosen for each of them. This left Huard, Mennefer, Bennem, and Mallie standing alone in front of me in the reception room, where a large chair of carved and polished oak had been placed. Here I would sit pompously and receive petitioners and visitors to my levees, at which a good part of the scheming, plotting, and backbiting that would surround my person would take place. I sat down, arranging my skirt into graceful folds and placing my hands on the carven arms of the chair.

"Well, Huard," I said quietly. "You might have mentioned to me that you intended to betray me."

"Only to your family, Eldrie Fitzroi. You saw how happy your brother was to see you. He was moved to tears!"

I snorted. "If you're going to live in a palace, you had better learn right now never to take any emotion at its face value, never to believe anything anyone tells you, and never, never turn your back, especially on your nearest and dearest. My brother is happy to see me, all right. He needs every little bit of political support for his claim to the throne he can get. My father is overjoyed to have me back; he has some use for me, though I don't know what it is yet. And the queen! Made her day, it did, having her husband's bastard come home and being forced to greet her with enthusiasm."

Huard bowed his head. "I'm sorry, Eldrie

Fitzroi. I had accepted the charge to find you and bring you home. It predated my oath to you by two years. That obligation is discharged now. My oath stands."

"What about the rest of you? Were you in on this?"

Bennem looked troubled. "Huard told us who you were, Eldrie Fitzroi. He explained that we could come with you because you'd be going home sooner than you thought. Mallie thought we ought to tell you, but I wouldn't let her. I was afraid you'd run away again, and we had wagered our whole future on you."

"Huard told me," Mennefer said. "I wouldn't— I wouldn't—I thought he belonged to you, so he told me who you were and that he was just— just—that because you were royal, you had a right to ask it of him, but it didn't mean any- thing and you wouldn't be hurt—"

"Damn you all," I whispered, sick to the depths of my heart. "Damn you all, I trusted you and I took your oaths and I tried to care for you as best I could. I thought you were my friends."

"We'll serve you loyally, Eldrie Fitzroi," Huard said. He was very pale. "I did what I thought was best. You're royal. You have re- sponsibilities; they need you here. No one has ever hired twenty Hunters to find a single per- son before."

I looked into his face. "Did you really think that I wouldn't be hurt? That it didn't mean anything to me when I came to you?"

Huard reached out and took Mennefer's hand. "I knew that you cared for me," he said, facing me squarely. "I knew you'd be hurt, a little. But I also knew that you didn't really love me. You

royal folk don't love people, not the way we
commoners love each other. I think, being truly
royal, you belong to all the people and can never
belong to just one. Your father can take as
many pretty favorites as he wants, and not be
bound as an ordinary man must be to one
woman. That's why what I said to Mennefer
about you was true. Being what you are, you
had a right to ask of me—of any man you desire—what you did, and I had to respond as I
did. But I couldn't go on being your lover. Remember what you said about the young farmer
yesterday? How would it have looked if I'd
brought you home as my mistress? I knew we
were coming here. Besides, I love Mennefer. I
didn't want to leave without her, knowing I was
committed to your service and wouldn't be
coming back. It was cruel, maybe, a little. But
it was a small cruelty to save a much greater
one. The only alternative I had was to tell you
the truth and bring you here by force."

I met his steady gaze. This time, he wasn't
lying to me. Slowly I nodded, and leaned back
in the chair, closing my eyes against the pain.
How very wrong he was, when he put himself
to one side of a line and my father and I on
another! There was no set of moral rules for
ordinary men and women and another for those
of royal birth! I had been wrong, wrong, wrong
to have gone to him as I had, and if only I had
known how he thought of me, how much bitter
humiliation could I have spared us both!

"A king's daughter has no more right to mis-
use a man for her pleasure than anyone else
does," I said. "Being royal is not a matter of
having the right to ignore the rules of conduct
that bind everyone else; it's having more re-

sponsibility and less freedom than ordinary people. It seems I have wronged you greatly, Huard."

There was a step and a hand touched mine, lifted it to soft lips. "Did you think I was unwilling? It was the greatest privilege of my life, and I was—I am—profoundly honored that you chose me. I've brought you back here against your will, to carry burdens you fled from home and family and royal privilege to avoid. If there were any way I could make the burdens lighter for you, I would. I was Huard the Hunter; from now on, I am Eldrie Fitzroi's liegeman."

"All right, Huard. I will hold you to your oath! All of you! We'll play out this game of politics and deceit and lies. You'll lie and cheat and scheme for me. Go make yourself at home in your new quarters, now. The next time I see you, I'll smile and speak to you politely, as I will all the other denizens of this gilded rat trap, no matter what's in my heart."

There was a subdued shuffle of feet, a muffled sob—Mennefer's, I supposed—and they were gone.

Felan came in and I rose and curtsied, schooling the feelings out of my face in the instant that my head was bowed.

"I'm glad you were kind to Uncle Joss," Felan said. "He was really hurt by the way you behaved to him before you left. You were a favorite with him too, you know."

"I was highly indignant that he was the queen's lover," I admitted ruefully. "Silly of me. If it hadn't been for him, I wouldn't have existed."

"I don't know about that," Felan said. "The king had a roving eye long before Uncle Joss showed up. Your mother was around for nearly a year before you were conceived, and Uncle Joss came a few weeks after your mother. There is some doubt as to whether I have any right to inherit the throne at all. I don't think even my mother knows for sure whose son I am. It's no help, of course, that I have none of the royal gifts."

"Faugh, royal gifts," I muttered. "I don't believe that there are any such things."

"Easy for you to say. How many ordinary girls of sixteen would go out into the world alone and come home trailing an entourage of their own liegemen?"

"That was no doing of mine. It was that damn Hunter you put on my trail."

"How many people of any sex or age could get a Hunter to offer them an oath? They don't break their oaths, Hunters don't. He could be a very valuable ally. You're going to need every friend you can get. Do you think this is going to be easy? Because of your birth and because you've been gone for sixteen years, who knows where, doing who knows what, you'll never be regarded by some people with the respect your efforts will deserve, especially after you're married to a commoner."

I choked. "Married?"

"Why, yes, of course. I need you to be married, as soon as possible."

"Why?"

"I wasn't supposed to be king, you know. But Jovian was so wild and reckless and so obviously unsuitable that maybe it wasn't a bad thing—well, anyway, here I am, heir, and I need all the help and support I can get."

"Father acknowledged you. I can't think why anyone would take exception to you, especially once you're married and have an heir of your own."

He colored. "Well, that's the problem. I can only love men," he said with some difficulty. "You have to give me an heir, Eldrie."

I stared at him. "Oh, Felan," I said at last, "how can you be king, then?"

"Someone has to be. And it didn't matter when I was only the younger prince—it was better, even, than if I had wanted to marry and raise a family of cousins to the rightful heirs. But now, people don't like knowing that the dynastic line will end when I die. There has to be an heir and the people will accept a son of yours. Otherwise there may be disaffection when the time comes for me to inherit. Besides, Father intends to use your marriage to bind a very important man to his service. Well, I'll let him tell you about that."

He glanced at me slyly to see what effect his news had upon me, but in the years since I had seen him last I had learned how not to let all my feelings show on my face. Disappointed, he sauntered out, leaving me more confounded than I had cared to let him see—this was my worse nightmare come true!

I sat in that carven chair with the new russet brocade upholstery for a long time and grieved. I mourned for my freedom and my youth and my profession—I had not been a great healer, no, but I had been a good healer, the best I knew how to be. I had saved lives, more than I lost, and I had eased suffering. There were many and many people in the world who were better for having had my help, babies I had birthed, oldsters at the end of their lives whose going had been easier because of me. Perhaps I wasn't a true princess, but how many princesses could say that?

And I had had my lovers—the bashful, eager youths and the merry scoundrels and the awkward ones amazed by passions they hardly understood. I had loved where my heart had led me, and sometimes I had made mistakes. But they had been my own mistakes. How many princesses could say that?

I had wandered wherever my fate guided me, and lived by my wits, well or poorly. I had seen mountains and desert and the great ocean in all its moods. I had lazed beneath the oaks of great forests and drifted like a lost dinghy across seas of grass. How many princesses could boast of as much?

And now I must turn from all of that to struggle in secret, smiling warfare among the great and powerful for those elusive intangibles of influence and prestige and national interest. This was not the life I would have chosen for myself. But who chooses their lives? We can only do our best with the positions we're born to and the gifts we're given. Perhaps I might, if I was very careful, escape with at least some small essential core of myself uncorrupted.

And very few princesses could say that.

Reading—
For The
Fun Of It

Ask a teacher to define the most important skill for success and inevitably she will reply, "the ability to read."

But millions of young people never acquire that skill for the simple reason that they've never discovered the pleasures books bring.

That's why there's RIF—Reading is Fundamental. The nation's largest reading motivation program. RIF works with community groups to get youngsters into books and reading. RIF makes it possible for young people to have books that interest them, books they can choose and keep. And RIF involves young people in activities that make them want to read—**for the fun of it.**

The more children read, the more they learn, and the more they **want** to learn.

There are children in your community—maybe in your own home—who need RIF. For more information, write to:

RIF
Dept. BK-3
Box 23444
Washington, D.C.
20026

Founded in 1966, RIF is a national, nonprofit organization with local projects run by volunteers in every state of the union.

OUTPASSAGE

JANET MORRIS & CHRIS MORRIS

It could have been the ultimate in blind dates,
but before Dennis Cox and Paige Barnett can
cement their mutual attraction for each other,
they are shanghaied to a backwater planet
where a fermenting rebellion threatens IST's
mining interests as well as the planet's existence. Drawn together in their mutual desire
for truth and justice, Dennis and Paige battle
the unknown in an epic adventure complete with
New Age space war, politics, and spirituality.

ISBN: 0-517-00832-7 $3.50

AN INTERSTELLAR EXPERIENCE

ON SALE NOW!